She was pregnant.

That was the first thing Officer Del Santini noticed as he approached the van he'd just pulled over. "Are you—"

"Any second now."

There was no time to call for help. Carefully Del lifted her into the rear of the van.

Melissa fought for consciousness. Every shred of energy, every ounce of concentration was focused on the pain.

His emergency training came back to Del as he watched the woman struggle to raise herself. "That's right. You're doing fine."

Del caught his breath as the crown of the baby's head appeared. He kept his voice calm, steady. "Push, Melissa. Push. C'mon, you can do it."

Melissa pushed again, feeling pain and release. A distant wail floated through the van.

Melissa fell back, tears of relief and joy mingling with the perspiration on her face. They had done it. Her baby was born.

MARIE FERRARELLA

Father Goose

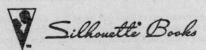

Published by Silhouette Books

America's Publisher of Contemporary Romance

SILHOUETTE BOOKS

ISBN 0-373-48348-1

FATHER GOOSE

Books by Marie Ferrarella

Silhouette Romance
The Gift #588
Five-Alarm Affair #613
Heart to Heart #632
Mother for Hire #686
Borrowed Baby #730
Her Special Angel #744
The Undoing of Justin
    Starbuck #766
Man Trouble #815
The Taming of the Teen #839
Father Goose #869
Babies on His Mind #920
The Right Man #932
In Her Own Backyard #947
Her Man Friday #959
Aunt Connie's Wedding #984
†Caution: Baby Ahead #1007
†Mother on the Wing #1026
†Baby Times Two #1037
Father in the Making #1078
The Women in Joe Sullivan's Life #1096
‡Do You Take This Child? #1145
The Man Who Would Be Daddy #1175
Your Baby or Mine? #1216

Silhouette Books
Silhouette Christmas Stories 1992
    "The Night Santa Claus Returned"

Fortune's Children
Forgotten Honeymoon

Silhouette Special Edition
It Happened One Night #597
A Girl's Best Friend #652
Blessing in Disguise #675
Someone To Talk To #703
World's Greatest Dad #767
Family Matters #832
She Got Her Man #843
Baby in the Middle #892
Husband: Some Assembly Required #931
Brooding Angel #963
‡Baby's First Christmas #997
Christmas Bride #1069
Wanted: Husband, Will Train #1132

Silhouette Desire
‡Husband: Optional #988

Silhouette Intimate Moments
*Holding Out for a Hero #496
*Heroes Great and Small #501
*Christmas Every Day #538
Callaghan's Way #601
*Caitlin's Guardian Angel #661
‡Happy New Year—Baby! #686
The Amnesiac Bride #787
Serena McKee's Back in Town #808

Silhouette Yours Truly
‡The 7lb., 2oz. Valentine
Let's Get Mommy Married
Traci on the Spot
Mommy and the Policeman Next Door

†Baby's Choice
‡The Baby of the Month Club
*Those Sinclairs

Books by Marie Ferrarella writing as Marie Nicole

Silhouette Desire
Tried and True #112
Buyer Beware #142
Through Laughter and Tears #161
Grand Theft: Heart #182
A Woman of Integrity #197
Country Blue #224
Last Year's Hunk #274
Foxy Lady #315
Chocolate Dreams #346
No Laughing Matter #382

Silhouette Romance
Man Undercover #373
Please Stand By #394
Mine by Write #411
Getting Physical #440

MARIE FERRARELLA

lives in Southern California. She describes herself as the tired mother of two overenergetic children and the contented wife of one wonderful man. The RITA Award-winning author is thrilled to be following her dream of writing full-time.

To Helen Conrad—
for listening (and listening, and
listening, and listening....

Chapter One

It was the kind of day that made Del Santini feel as if he was moving in slow motion, even though he was riding along at fifty-five miles an hour on the Newport Freeway. In his white police-issue helmet and stiff black boots, he was sure the temperature had risen above the projected ninety-three degrees.

Dry heat was better than humidity, he thought philosophically. And any perspiration that was generated by the weather and his required gear quickly evaporated as he guided his motorcycle in and out of the afternoon traffic.

He grinned to himself. It wasn't all that long ago that he had been counting the months until he was old enough to legally ride a motorcycle. Now he couldn't wait to stop riding one and find a nice, air-conditioned room where he could relax and unwind. He sighed. There were still three more hours left to his shift before he could do anything about turning his longing into a reality.

A loud rattling noise grew louder just behind him to the left. Del heard the old van a few seconds before he saw it. The vehicle, with a large dent on the passenger side, streaked by him in the inside car-pool lane like a silver bullet, hurtling toward some distant target.

Del immediately snapped to attention, his lethargy vanishing as if it had never existed. The van was doing at least seventy-five.

The audacity of some people never ceased to amaze Del. He hadn't hidden himself behind a sign on a lonesome highway with nothing but empty miles stretching out before the motorist. Del was zipping along on his motorcycle, all six foot four of him, hardly a sight easily missed. The motorist had to have seen him as he shot by. Either the driver didn't care if the police saw him speeding, or it was worth the risk.

Well, Del would find out soon enough.

Flipping on the hypnotic blue and red lights, Del went through motions that were second nature to him now. Considering the hefty fine levied for going an estimated twenty miles over the speed limit, the van's driver had to be in one hell of a hurry. Either that or stupid.

He also wasn't using his mirrors, Del concluded, annoyed as he trailed after the van. The vehicle hadn't slowed an iota since he had switched on his lights. Increasing his speed to eighty, Del turned on his siren.

Shifting into the right lane, he sped past a man in a tan car.

Del began to entertain the idea that the person in the van might be dangerous. Why else would he continue speeding? He was about to call in for backup when the van finally slowed down, then stopped smack in the middle of the lane. Cars swerved out of the way to avoid a collision. Choice words formed in Del's mind about the extent of the driver's intelligence.

Pulling up to the van on the passenger side, Del looked in. There was only one occupant, a woman. Was she crazy? he thought. Did she have any idea of the size of the penalty for using the car-pool lane when she was traveling by herself?

"Pull over!" he shouted through the open window.

The woman turned her head and looked at him. Young, he thought. She would probably be pretty if she didn't look so terribly worn. Her dark hair was pulled back in a careless ponytail at the nape of her neck. Even from here he could see that she was very pale. Her expression was slightly dazed. She looked stunned. No, in a trance would be a better description. He wondered if she was on drugs.

Melissa Ryan pulled air into her lungs to steady herself and fight back the panic that was building. The air felt too hot. It didn't help. Oh, God. Why was the policeman shouting at her? "What?"

"Pull over!" he commanded more sharply. He waved his hand at the shoulder of the road. "You're blocking traffic."

Punctuating his statement, a car screeched not more than twenty feet away, switching lanes at the last minute. Del stifled a curse. He had to get this woman over before he had a multicar pileup on his hands. He was just grateful that it was early afternoon and traffic wasn't heavy yet.

Watching her, Del saw the woman inside the van bite down on her lower lip before she turned the wheel sharply to the left, drawing the van onto the shoulder of the road as best she could.

Satisfied that they were out of harm's way, Del got off his motorcycle and shook his head. He wondered where the woman had been hiding when brains were being handed out. He pulled out his ticket book. The fine for traveling in the car-pool lane alone was upward of two hundred dollars. For openers. Judging by the condition of the van, she probably couldn't afford the penalty. Why did people do these stupid things?

Wearily he wondered what sort of a bill of goods she'd try to sell him. On the force for four years, he had heard all kinds of stories and explanations as motorists tried to talk their way out of having traffic tickets served on them.

"Lady," he began, bracing himself for dramatic pleas as he walked around to her side of the van, "there's only one of you in the car."

Sweat was dripping into Melissa's eyes as she fought to maintain control and keep the pain at bay. She blinked, one hand clutching the steering wheel. Her knuckles were white. "Not for long," she bit off.

It was then that he noticed.

She was pregnant. So pregnant, Del didn't understand how he could have missed the fact when he had first looked in. Seeing her now, he had no idea how she had managed to get herself behind the steering wheel. It looked like an incredibly tight fit. The sternness left his voice. "Are you—"

Melissa nodded without turning toward him. "Any second now."

She couldn't move. The pain was almost making her light-headed. It had been a mistake to try to drive herself to the hospital. But there had been no one to ask, and the contractions had started coming. She had looked up the address of the closest hospital and gotten into the van, praying she wouldn't get lost.

Del looked around in the back of the van for another occupant, unable to believe that she was driving by herself in this condition. But there was no one else in the vehicle.

His attention was suddenly jerked back to the woman as she grabbed his hand and held on, hard. For someone who, except for the rounded mound before her, looked so small and delicate, she had one hell of a grip. A little gasp escaped her lips involuntarily.

"Easy now." His voice was soft as he covered her hand with his other. He felt what he thought was a wedding ring beneath his fingers. Damn, where was her husband at a time like this? "Is this your first one?"

Melissa's lips were dry, and she licked them before she could manage an answer. "Yes." It was hard to

concentrate on anything but the pain that was engulfing her, even as it ebbed away.

Del summoned the most positive, reassuring smile
he could muster. He was the second in a family of
six and had absorbed a few details along the way. His
younger sister had thought she was in labor three
times before the actual event happened.

"There's time." Del squeezed her hand as he
looked into eyes the color of deep chocolate. "First
babies always take a long time."

That's what her doctor in Arizona had told her, but
it didn't feel that way. She was certain it was going
to happen now, in a hurry.

"Tell the baby that. I don't think he knows." She
splayed her other hand over the top of her stomach
protectively. "He thinks he's supposed to put in an
appearance." Another sharp pain crashed into her
consciousness without warning. She clutched Del's
hand harder. *"Now."*

He didn't know how to make her feel better and
fervently wished for a veteran officer at his side, one
who had been through this sort of thing before. All
he had to draw on was a classroom exercise and
words in a textbook he couldn't quite remember.
"There's nothing to worry about until your water
breaks."

Melissa turned as the pain edged away for a second, giving her a slight reprieve. "Then start worry-
ing. It broke half an hour ago."

She wasn't just being panicky. This was serious.

He tried to disengage himself from her death grip. "In that case, I'd better radio for help."

But she wouldn't let go of his hand. She felt if she did, she'd be lost. "There's—no—time." The words came in breathy gasps.

God, she was so scared. She'd known it was going to hurt, but she hadn't thought that she'd be alone, in the middle of a strange city. She had pictured it all so differently. Alan was supposed to be here, holding her hand, telling her he loved her.

But Alan was gone. And so was everything else.

She looked at the policeman. She had no right to ask, but she needed someone. And his eyes were kind. She hated begging, but her pride had long since gone, washed away in the tide of physical pain that overtook her.

"Please, don't leave me. I—" The next word was muffled as she stifled a small cry.

There had been a training course at the academy, but Del had never actually delivered a baby before. Apprehension filled him. What if something went wrong? What if he— Del looked at the woman's face. Even wreathed in pain, she looked to be no more than twenty-two or -three. She was obviously frightened. How could he be thinking of himself at a time like this? This woman needed him, perhaps more than anyone had ever needed him before. It was up to him to help her in any way he could.

He wrapped his fingers around her hand. "I'm not leaving."

Melissa managed a weak smile of gratitude in return. All her energy was devoted to trying to breathe.

He had no options available to him. Once again he wished for a partner. But it was too late for that. "Do you think you can manage to get into the back?" He nodded toward the interior of the van.

The pain had mercifully subsided for a moment. She loosened her hold on his hand. "That's what got me into all this."

Del looked at her, confused. "What?"

She shook her head. "Poor joke."

A joke.

That was all that it was now. Just a poor joke. Once, it had made for a wonderful memory. She had planned to tell the child whose heart beat beneath her own that it had been conceived while she and Alan had gone camping. Vividly she would have recreated the scene, saying how it had started raining suddenly and she and the baby's father had taken shelter in the van before they had a chance to put up the tent. It had been a wonderful night, the sound of steady rain beating on the outside of the van, Alan holding her close, telling her he loved her.

But like all memories, it was in the past. Just as Alan was.

Biting down on her lip, Melissa turned in her seat, easing herself out from beneath the steering wheel. She rose unsteadily, still holding on to Del's hand.

Del leaned forward to keep his arm from being pulled out of its socket. He couldn't follow her in. "Um, you're going to have to let go of my hand."

She looked up at him, confused for a moment, then flushed, letting go. Stupid. She was acting stupid. She had to get a hold of herself. She had been in a daze since yesterday morning, after discovering Alan's note. It was to have been her wedding day. Instead all she held in her hand was a note. And now this was happening. The baby wasn't supposed to be due until the beginning of next month. Too soon. It was too soon, she wasn't ready.

"Oh, sorry." She opened her hand and then clenched it again, as if gripping herself for strength.

Del wondered if it was a habit. Did she have anyone to lean on, or was she used to being on her own? He could see no other explanation for her driving herself to the hospital.

He climbed into the van right behind her, surprisingly agile for such a tall man. It was something his sister Kathleen had remarked on more than once, teasing him that he should have sought a career with the Joffrey Ballet instead of Newport Beach's police force.

The van closed in on her, narrowing down to almost a pinpoint. Melissa swayed, fighting for consciousness. The next thing she knew, the policeman was surrounding her, holding her in his arms. There was something very protective in the way he held her. She let him comfort her, knowing she had no right, knowing it meant less than nothing.

His face, inches from hers, looked at her in concern. "Are you all right?"

The darkness faded, allowing the sunlight to come

into the van. She smiled weakly as she leaned against him. "I've been better."

Del looked around uncertainly, his natural ability to take charge in danger of evaporating. "I don't know about this." He looked toward the front of the van. "If I just call in—"

She was about to agree when there was another fierce tightening through her body. It was going to be a matter of minutes now, she just knew it. She wound her fingers into anything she could find. His shirt was the closest thing available. "There isn't time."

He didn't miss the barely controlled panic. "You know best."

"Just this once," she murmured, more to herself than to him, thinking of all the things she should have done differently.

He hardly heard her. His mind raced around, trying to recall everything they had taught him about delivering a child. He remembered teasing Dennis, his brother-in-law, when Dennis had turned green the first time Kathy had mentioned having him in the delivery room. This was nature's way of getting even with him, Del thought ruefully. He made a mental note to apologize to Dennis the first opportunity he got.

Del saw a blanket shoved in one corner of the van. "Can you stand by yourself?" He looked at her uncertainly.

Bracing one arm on the back of the driver's seat, Melissa nodded. Del let go and quickly grabbed the blanket. As the woman sagged, he braced her with one arm and haphazardly spread out the blanket on the floor with the other. It was the best he could do.

At least the floor of the van was carpeted and well padded, he noted.

It had served as their bed when they moved cross-country from Georgia. Melissa remembered when they had bought it. A used-car salesman had given them "a deal." Enamored with the idea of traveling, Alan had said yes immediately. There had been some good times in the van to be savored. And some bad. The repair bills alone had amounted to more than the van had cost them. Alan had only said, "Don't sweat the small stuff." She hadn't realized then that that was his philosophy about all of life.

Melissa was surprised that Alan had left the van when he ran off. But even he couldn't have driven two cars at once, she thought. And the Mustang had been the newer of the two. And the faster.

She squeezed her eyes shut as another contraction seized her. Melissa started to breathe hard, afraid to push, afraid not to. She was suddenly aware that the policeman was easing her down onto something dark.

Navy. The carpet wasn't navy. It was a light rose. The blanket, he was setting her down on the blanket. His hands were gentle, kind. They were so large, how could they be so gentle as well?

She was drifting. She had to stay conscious. Oh God, this hurt.

Her baby was going to be born here, with cars honking at one another and a world whizzing just a few feet away. On the 55 Freeway. It wasn't much of a beginning to offer. And she had had such hopes. Dreams. But dreams faded when you were awake.

Melissa arched her back as another contraction rippled into the last one. It felt like a clenched fist, holding her in its power.

Holding, holding, and then finally releasing her.

Sweat poured out of her, plastering her hair against her forehead. Letting go of the breath she had been holding, Melissa realized that her eyes had been squeezed shut and that she had held on to the policeman with both hands, clutching at his arm. There was a tear at the top of the sleeve and a fresh scratch along his forearm.

"Did I do that?"

He wanted to keep her mind off the pain, if that was possible. He glanced at the sleeve. "I think that comes under the heading of civilian brutality." He grinned, brushing the hair from her forehead. It was a surprisingly intimate gesture. "You're pretty strong for such a little thing."

She rested her hand on her stomach, wishing herself past this. She felt heavy, clumsy. Ugly. "I'm not so little."

But she was. Small and petite. She looked too fragile to be having this baby. "Have it your way. I make it a point never to argue with pregnant women."

Was he talking about his wife? she wondered. Did he have a family with a lot of children? Did they look like him? Would hers look like her? Or would she look down into the small face and see Alan?

"Are you married?" Melissa's question rushed out in a pant.

He gave her his hand to hang on to, wishing he could do more. "Nope." Her hold was so tight he thought that perhaps she was breaking his fingers. "What do you want?"

Melissa seemed to sink deeper into the blanket, gathering her strength for the next onslaught. "For this to be over."

He laughed softly. "No, I meant do you want a boy or a girl?"

Once it hadn't mattered. Now it did. She turned her face toward the blanket. "A boy. I want a boy so he'll never hurt."

Del took out his handkerchief and lightly wiped her brow. "The pain'll be over soon."

Melissa turned to look at him. His features swam before her. "I didn't mean childbirth. I meant lov-*ing*." The word ended in a shriek as another contraction came, harder, faster than the other.

She started panting. It was what she had seen others do in the movies. Alan hadn't wanted to go to a childbirth class and, somehow, she had let the opportunity slip by. She had fooled herself into thinking there would be time when they were married and settled.

Del felt helpless. There wasn't anything he could do except make her comfortable and give her someone to hold on to. She had the last part down pat, he thought as her nails dug into his hand again.

Her eyes looked glazed over. The contractions were coming almost on top of each other, Del thought. The

baby was going to be born any second now. He
wished that there were clean sheets around her. And
water to wash his hands. Most of all, he wished he
had been able to get her to a hospital. They were only
five miles away from one of the best hospitals in
southern Orange County.

They may as well have been a hundred miles away
for all the good it did.

He watched as she tried to relax the tension in her
body. "I think you're going to be a mother very
soon."

The man was a genius. "I think so, too." She
flushed, an apologetic look coming over her. She
hadn't meant to be sarcastic. "Oh, God...I feel
like...someone...is using me...for a wishbone."

He saw her arch again. There was no more time to
waste. Del extracted his hand from hers and moved
to the end that was going to require all his attention
for the next few minutes.

He looked at the woman and gave her an encouraging smile. "My name is Del Santini." Taking a
breath, he picked up the hem of the light green caftan
she was wearing. "I thought you might want to know
before I get a hell of a lot more personal than I expected to when I pulled you over."

She dug her fingertips into the blanket, wadding it
frantically beneath her hands, trying desperately not
to scream, barely aware that he had pushed her dress
up around her waist.

"Melissa." The name was forced out of her mouth
by sheer willpower. "Melissa—" she repeated. She

couldn't summon the strength to say her last name. Every shred of energy, every ounce of concentration she had left was focused on the pain searing through her loins. And the cause of it.

Sweat was beading up on his brow and sliding out of every pore in his body. His uniform felt heavy and miserably damp as it stuck to him.

Please, God, don't let it be a breech baby. Things began to come back to him. "Melissa, can you try to sit up? Just pull your elbows in against your body and raise yourself up a little." He watched as she struggled to do as he told her. "That's right. You're doing fine." *Let's hope I can do fine, too.*

He pulled in his breath as the crown of the baby's head appeared. Del felt his heart race. "I see the head, Melissa. The baby's almost here." Exercising maximum control, he kept his voice calm, steady, something for her to hang on to. "Now push, Melissa. Push."

Concentrating, she squeezed the muscles of her body. She was afraid she was going to pass out from the pain, and fought to stay conscious. It was so horribly stifling in the van. There was no air, nothing to breathe. She thought her lungs might explode—along with the rest of her.

She began to feel as if she had been doing this for hours instead of just minutes. She'd heard stories of labor that went on for hours, for days. When she had climbed into the van earlier, she'd thought she'd have enough time to reach the hospital.

But there was no time. It was happening all too

fast. Everything was happening too fast. Happiness had fled too quickly.

Del's voice broke through, bringing her back.

"Push, Melissa, push."

She gasped for air, cursing him in her mind. "I'm pushing, I'm pushing." She squeezed again, then stopped, drained. "He won't come."

Just a little more, he thought, frustrated. How could his mother have gone through this six times? It was madness, enduring this kind of pain. "He's trying. You try with him."

The man was heartless. "Anyone ever tell you you're obnoxious?" The words came out in angry pants.

He kept his eyes on the dark crown. The baby would be born with hair. "Lots of people. When this is over, we'll go over the list."

Del raised his head. Perspiration shone on her face. She looked exhausted beyond description. Damn, why didn't another policeman come by and see his motorcycle outside the van? Where was a policeman when you needed him? he thought sarcastically. "Don't faint on me now, Melissa, I can't do this alone."

She let her head fall forward, her chin hitting her chest.

Del tried not to panic. "Melissa?"

Melissa jerked up her head. "I'm trying, I'm trying." Squeezing her eyes shut, she strained and pushed again as hard as she could until she thought that she was being turned inside out.

"The head's out!" Del was filled with wonder as he cradled the tiny head between his large hands.

"What—is—it?"

"I can't tell by the ears. You have to give me more to work with. One more push, Melissa." He knew pushing the baby's shoulders out was the hardest part. "Just one more."

One more. Just one more. She was going to die with those words ringing in her ears. "Easy for you to say," she gasped, straining.

"Not at the moment." He wished he could mop the sweat from her forehead. She was drenched and seemed to be getting weaker by the second. He tried to get her angry. Anger worked where kindness didn't sometimes. "C'mon, c'mon," he urged gruffly. "Women are doing this all over the world. You can do it."

Her head swirling, she saw him through a haze and knew that he was trying anything he could to keep her conscious. She was so exhausted, all she wanted to do was collapse. Why couldn't he just let her collapse?

Drawing her elbows in tightly against her body until she was almost pinching her sides, Melissa pushed again. If the baby wasn't born this time, she knew she was going to die.

A distant wail floated through the van.

A siren.

No, a baby. Her baby.

Melissa fell back against the blanket, tears of relief and joy mingling with the perspiration on her face. They had done it.

Chapter Two

It was a humbling experience to hold a new life in his hands. Del was speechless. For a precious moment, he felt as if he was suddenly apart from the scene, watching it transpire at a distance. Seeing the tiny baby, even covered with blood and a cheesy substance over her small face, left him in utter awe.

The baby made one protesting whimper at being forced to leave the warm shelter she had known these past few months and then became silent. Her almost iridescently blue eyes were opened wide, and staring straight at him. He knew it was impossible, but she seemed to be studying him, as if she wanted to know who this man was who was the first to hold her in this brand-new world.

Del knew he was a goner from that moment on.

"What is it?" Melissa breathed deeply. She needed more oxygen to still the fierce pounding of her heart.

She had never felt this completely depleted in her life. Why wasn't the baby making any more noise? "Is it all right?" New panic fed on the old and she had no strength for either. "The baby isn't crying."

"It's a girl." Del turned the newly minted little person toward her so that Melissa could see for herself. "And she's too busy looking to cry." His voice cracked a little. He stopped talking. God, he was grateful that they were both all right. He didn't know if he could have withstood the guilt if something had gone wrong.

The baby had what looked to be cream cheese scattered on her face. "What's on her face?"

"It wipes off," he told her. To prove it, he ran the tip of his finger along the baby's cheek, then held it up. "See?" He recalled something he had once heard. "My mother said that babies born with a caul are meant to be lucky."

Lucky. With no father and a mother who had no money, no job, no place to stay. That didn't spell luck in her book. Melissa struggled with an overwhelming sense of despair. The baby was alive. That was all that mattered. She was too tired to think any further than that.

Del placed the baby on the blanket. Her blue eyes seemed to follow him. Watching the tiny face, he dug into his pants pocket, looking for the Swiss army knife his father had given him the summer before he died. A smile lifted the corners of his mouth as his fingers curled around the object. The man probably never would have thought, when he handed the prize to his anxious twelve-year-old son, that someday Del would be using it to cut an umbilical cord in the back of a '78 van.

Sunlight reflected on the shiny metal blade, creating a point of light that performed a dance on the wall of the van. Melissa's pulse quickened.

"What are you doing?" She watched as Del flipped on his pocket lighter and passed it slowly over the blade.

Satisfied that he had gotten all of the blade, he closed the lighter. No sense in taking chances. "I've got to cut the cord."

Melissa winced as another contraction suddenly seized her body. Wasn't it ever going to be over? "Del?"

Immediately his eyes shifted from the tiny life at his knees to Melissa's face. It was etched in startled surprise. And pain. "What?"

"It's starting again. I can't be having another one—can I?" She looked down at her stomach in horror. "The doctor didn't say anything about twins."

He made a calculated guess, surprised at how much of his course he did remember. "It's the placenta," he told her, sounding a good deal more calm than he felt. "It's got to come out, too."

Within moments, that too was expelled. Holding his breath and muttering a fragment of a prayer he had learned during his childhood, when prayers had been important, he cut the cord.

That done, he let out a long breath and folded his knife, never taking his eyes off the baby. He had nothing to clean her with and nothing to wrap around her tiny body. Hesitating only for a moment, he stripped off his shirt, then tucked it around the tiny miracle. Carefully, using a corner of his shirt, he wiped her face. The baby wrinkled her face and he laughed.

"Here." He picked the baby up and gently set the bundle into Melissa's arms. "I'm afraid it's the best that I can do." He nodded at the shirt. "Not even swaddling clothes."

"Dark blue's her color," Melissa murmured, looking down into the tiny face of her daughter. Her daughter. It didn't seem possible. And yet it was true. Gratitude flooded through her veins, mingling with relief. "I don't know how to thank you."

Del shrugged and grinned. "I'd say 'all in a day's work,' except that I've never had a day like this before." Still on his knees, Del passed his hand lightly over the baby's head. She had dark hair, like her mother, he thought.

A broad, beefy face peered in through the passenger's window. "Everything all right in here?" The deep-set gray eyes squinted as the man recognized Del. "Hey, Del, is that you?"

Del's head jerked up, momentarily disoriented. "Larry." It took a few beats before he could pull his thoughts together. For a little while there, it had felt as if the world did not extend beyond Melissa, the baby and himself. "Man, am I glad to see you."

Larry took in the woman on the blanket and the bare-chested young officer kneeling right above her. He shook his head slowly. "Well, you should be. If

I had been any other officer, catching you getting a little afternoon delight—''

Del stared at the man who had taken him under his wing when he first came to work at the precinct, utterly confused. ''What?''

And then he looked down, realizing that Larry was frowning disapprovingly at his bare chest. The tension that had mounted only a few minutes ago left him in a rush. Del laughed and rocked back on his heels.

''No, Larry. She just had a baby.'' Del looked at the little girl who appeared to be silently regarding him. Unable to resist, he took the tiny fist in his. So small, so soft. He raised his eyes and saw that Melissa was watching him.

Larry shook his bald head. ''Aren't you supposed to wait a couple of months or something? My wife said—''

Obviously it had been a long, hard day for all of them. ''*Now,* Larry.'' Del gestured around. ''She just had the baby now. Here, in the van. You missed it by no more than two minutes.''

The older policeman opened the door and eased himself inside the van. He angled his body past the seat and into the back. ''Hey, no kidding?'' The expression on his round, wide face softened immediately and became infinitely respectful as he looked at Melissa. ''Are you all right, ma'am?''

He looked like a huge, towering tree trunk from where she lay on the floor. ''I am, thanks to him.'' She smiled at Del.

Fifteen years on the force kicked in and Larry went

on automatic pilot. "We'd better get you to a hospital." Larry glanced at Del, still kneeling next to Melissa. Sweat gleamed on the upper part of the younger man's torso. "And you into uniform." With a wide palm outspread, Larry gestured for Del to remain where he was. "Wait right here, I'll radio this in and then drive the van. You stay with her and make sure nothing happens to them." He grinned foolishly at the baby. "Baby okay?"

Del still held the tiny fist in his. "Perfect from where I sit."

Larry nodded. "Good." He left them for a moment to call in.

The baby fussed a little. Del tucked his shirt more securely around the small legs. His fingers accidentally brushed against Melissa's breast. He dropped his hand, trying not to be obvious. Their eyes met for a moment. Hers were filled with pain, a different sort of pain than anything physical could generate.

A multitude of feelings and emotions spilled through him, so many and so fast that he couldn't begin to sort them out. He just knew that they were all centered around the tiny little lady he had brought into the world.

And the woman who was holding her.

Startled at his thoughts, Del reined them in. He couldn't let himself get emotionally involved. She was a married woman. As free-spirited as he was in his relationships, he had certain ironclad rules. Rules he never broke, no matter what.

He had a feeling a test was coming up.

He forced himself back into the role of public servant. What had happened, as unusual as it was for him, was all supposed to be in the line of duty. Only the feelings weren't. But that was his problem, not hers. "I'll notify your husband as soon as we get to the hospital."

Melissa deliberately concentrated on the life in her arms. Fresh tears threatened to sting her eyes. Except that this time they wouldn't be tears of relief. "That won't be easy."

He heard the sadness in her voice. Was she just exhausted by her ordeal? Or was it something more? "Is he away?"

She wished he'd stop asking her questions. She hadn't the strength for this now. She didn't want to tell him that the ring on her finger was something she had bought herself to ward off curious stares when she had grown noticeably pregnant. That there was no husband, only a man who didn't love her enough to stay.

His words were flat, devoid of emotion and all the more powerful for it. "Well, maybe—"

She felt her temper about to snap. Why couldn't he leave her alone? Melissa struggled with her emotions. Why was she so irritated with this man who had just done so much for her? "I don't know where he is."

Had her husband left her? He didn't understand. How could anyone leave his wife just when she was about to give birth? Del wanted to touch her face, to soothe away the furrow that had creased her brow.

But he kept his hand at his side. It wasn't his place to be personal.

"We could find him," he offered softly, knowing that he would put out the APB on the man himself and not fully knowing why.

Melissa turned her face toward Del. Fierce determination came into her eyes, generated by hurt, anger and all the emotions Alan's disappearance had raised.

"I don't want him found. *He* doesn't want to be found." Tears began to fall and she hated herself for it. Hated the policeman who made her think of this. She'd promised herself not to cry again, not to waste tears over Alan when he wasted no thoughts on her. But she was too physically drained to be strong emotionally.

"Please." Melissa placed her hand on his in supplication. "I don't want to talk about him."

Now that she wasn't clutching at him in pain, her fingers felt light, cool on his. Yet something warm and passionate was happening to Del. A bonding he had never quite experienced before, despite all the women he had known and made love with. This was something unique, different. He suspected that it was because of what they had shared.

"Then we won't." Del looked toward the front of the van. Larry was climbing into the driver's seat. Within moments, the other policeman was driving them to the hospital at top speed.

"Don't you worry, little momma." Larry tossed the words over his shoulder. "We'll have you at the hospital in no time flat. The dispatcher is radioing ahead to let them know we're coming. They'll take care of you and the baby one, two, three."

Melissa looked up at the dark-haired man next to her. The stranger who had come to her aid. Lightly she placed her hand on his bare arm and smiled. "I've already been taken care of, Officer," she said softly.

Incredible fatigue suddenly overtook her. She was physically exhausted and still emotionally over-wrought after yesterday. Melissa fell asleep without even knowing that she closed her eyes.

The commotion around her woke Melissa a few minutes later. There were voices coming from all directions, hands lifting her, putting her down on something. A sheet was thrown over her and she felt herself in motion.

Her arms felt empty.

"My baby?" Melissa cried before she even opened her eyes.

"Right here."

She turned and saw the policeman—Del, she re-membered—hurrying along next to her. She was on a gurney and they were going through electronic doors, into the hospital. Del pointed to Melissa's left where a nurse held her baby, now wrapped in a white hospital blanket.

"The baby's fine," he assured her in a voice that was low and patient. "She's being taken care of."

Taken care of. Everything was being taken care of. Melissa drifted back to sleep with the sound of Del's voice in her head, feeling safe the way she had when she was a very young child.

"We'll take it from here. Thanks." One of the orderlies moved in front of Del. It was only then that he realized he had taken her hand again. He released it, then stood and watched as the team of orderlies continued to wheel Melissa down the pastel-colored corridor.

Someone cleared their throat behind him. He turned to see a young woman holding a clipboard and eyeing his bare chest with more than a smidgen of interest. "Would either of you two officers know if the lady has any medical coverage?"

Del remembered the purse he had grabbed when the orderlies were lifting Melissa out of the van. There had to be some information about insurance there.

Maybe he'd even discover a photograph of the husband she didn't want found.

Del pushed away the thought. Not his business. "Yeah, she has coverage." He had no idea if Melissa did or not, but she'd been through enough for one day. If she didn't have insurance, he'd find a way to make some sort of arrangements for her.

As Larry stood and watched, Del opened Melissa's purse. Though her life appeared to be in a state of turmoil for the moment, the woman was apparently incredibly neat. Her purse was in complete order. There were no wadded up tissues, no loose change, no forgotten receipts or ticket stubs tossed in. Just a comb, a lipstick and a wallet.

Within the wallet, the bills, what there were of them, were all arranged in descending order and facing forward. Del found an identification card issued by a prominent insurance company next to an Arizona driver's license. He noted that her last name was Ryan.

"Here." He thrust the card at the woman who sighed in relief.

That resolved, the woman allowed herself another brief moment to appreciate the shirtless policeman in front of her. Del heard Larry stifle a laugh. This wasn't the first time they'd encountered an appreciative woman. The woman smiled broadly. Invitingly. "If you'll follow me."

The swinging doors at the other end of the hallway closed, cutting off his view of Melissa and her baby. That part of his job was over. Or so Del tried to convince himself.

"Might as well," he muttered. Larry didn't follow him as he went to the admissions desk.

Del had just finished reading off the information on Melissa's identification card to the woman when Larry returned and walked up behind him. "Here."

Del turned and took the dark material the other man thrust at him. "What's this?"

"I had Mahoney bring over an extra shirt for you. The captain doesn't like his men to make like Tarzan around the civilians." Del shrugged into the shirt. "It shakes their confidence."

"Doesn't shake mine," the woman behind the desk

murmured under her breath as she keyed in the last of the information Del had given her.

Larry laughed and patted his ever-growing stomach, a trace of wistfulness in his eyes. "Oh, to be young again." He laid a heavy hand on Del's shoulder. "You about ready to go?"

"I'm finished here."

Del rose as he closed the remaining button on the dark blue shirt. Shoving the ends into the waistband of his slacks, he began to follow Larry to the automatic front doors. Then he stopped and looked down the corridor where Melissa had been taken. He turned to the woman behind the desk. "Do you think I might be able to see her now?"

The woman's smile was sympathetic as well as envious. "I think she'd like her rest for a while. But visiting hours are until eight if you'd like to come back."

Yes, Del thought, he would. He told himself it was just to check on her progress. It wasn't every day a man got to deliver a baby.

"C'mon, Father Goose, I'll take you back to your motorcycle." Larry took hold of Del's arm and tugged him toward the exit.

Del fell into step next to him, grinning. The doors slid open for them, then closed again as they walked through. He suddenly realized what a gorgeous day it was. The air from the not too distant sea was stirring the tops of the trees. It felt great to be alive. "Hey, Lar?"

Larry turned form his squad car. "What?"

"I delivered my first baby today."

Larry merely shook his head and laughed. "Yeah, I know."

The sheets were freshly starched and felt cool and comforting against her body. The preset thermostat on the wall saw to it that the temperature in the room was a moderate seventy-three degrees while outside the window, the world roasted. An orderly had come in earlier to bring her dinner and then had returned to sweep it away half an hour later. A nurse had massaged her aching back and another had brought her baby to her and kindly taken the infant to the nursery when Melissa had grown tired again.

Everything was being done for her. Everything was being taken care of.

Melissa had never felt so lost, so horribly alone in her life.

She turned and stared at the single beige curtain at the window next to her. Beige. Almost devoid of color. Like her life.

Now what? she thought, fighting back despair. Now what? What was she going to do, with a baby depending on her? Except for what was in her wallet, she had no money, no job and no place to stay.

Hot tears sprang up to her eyes again. She rubbed them away with the back of her hand, annoyed with herself for falling to pieces this way. It wasn't like her. She'd always been the one to take lemons and make lemonade. Each and every time.

But this time, oh, this time she felt she was stand-

ing in front of a huge mountain that blocked out the
sun for her. There was daylight on the other side, she
knew there was, but she was much too tired to climb
up to it. Finally too tired.

A bitter smile twisted her lips. Pollyana was sur-
rendering. Alan had done that to her, sapped away
her last bit of energy, her last bit of hope. She
couldn't hope anymore.

He had run off and taken everything but the van
and her clothes, leaving only a note in his wake. After
almost a year, there was only a note to mark the fact
that their lives had touched.

A note and a baby.

In the note he had said that she could always get
by on her brains. He needed an edge. He knew she'd
understand, so he was taking the money and the car.
That was it. Nothing else. He hadn't even bothered
to wish her luck. What she had mistaken for love on
his part had just been laziness. He hadn't the energy
to move on alone. Until now.

Brains. He said she had brains. A sad smile played
on her lips. If she truly had had brains, she wouldn't
have let this happen to her. She would have realized
that love *was* blind, at least in her case. Her love had
made her blind enough to overlook Alan's faults.

Melissa dragged her hand through her hair, frustrated. He had seemed so wonderfully carefree when
she had met him in Georgia. He was handsome and
fun and hadn't been intimidated by the fact that she
was so much brighter than he was. To her relief, he'd

made light of it and said that she was the brains of the operation. He was the beauty.

But beauty was only skin-deep.

His emotions, his sense of responsibility, had been only skin-deep as well. They had run no further than the surface, as shallow as his promises. If she hadn't been so in love, so awed about *being* in love, she would have realized it.

In the distance, she heard the cry of a sea gull. It made her feel lonelier.

How could she have been such an idiot?

Because Alan had made it so easy to believe in him. And she had wanted to. Wanted to believe that the American dream was hers for the asking. Alan had even been excited about the baby when she had told him she was pregnant. He'd made plans with her, wonderful plans and it had all seemed so rosy. So perfect, even in that furnished one-room apartment in Arizona. He'd promised to marry her as soon as things "came together" for him. But they never did.

And soon the excitement waned as work and the pregnancy had sapped her strength. She'd stayed home at night while he still went out with his friends, still had a good time. *Always* had a good time. And she had been left to pick up the pieces.

Melissa sighed as she ran her hands up and down her arms, suddenly cold. She had to stop feeling sorry for herself. She had a brand-new life depending on her. There was no time to wallow in self-pity.

Well, maybe just a little, she relented. Just for to-night.

Tomorrow, she promised herself, she was going to figure things out and see what she could do. There had to be a way to get back on her feet again. She wasn't down and out yet. She wasn't going to end up like her mother had, sitting in an institution, too depressed by life to even move until she finally died.

Come the fall, she would get back into teaching. Her teaching credentials only qualified her to teach in Arizona, but that could be worked out. She could take courses at the local college and—

Melissa sighed. She was thinking of the distant future. September. An eternity away. It was *now* that was the problem. Now and tomorrow and the next day and the one after that. Two mouths to feed and a roof to be provided overhead without sacrificing any more of her pride than had already been lost.

How on earth was she supposed to manage that? She had no magic up her sleeve. There was no one back home in Georgia to turn to. Both her parents were long since gone and her aunt and uncle had three sons to finish raising. She couldn't very well just turn up on their doorstep like someone in an old-fashioned melodrama, baby in her arms, asking for shelter.

Melissa pulled her knees up to her chest, as if that would give her the strength she needed. No, she had to do this on her own. Somehow, someway, it had to be on her own. The way it always had been.

Except, she thought wearily, she didn't know anyone she could turn to. Especially not here. She was new in southern California. Alan's wanderlust had prompted him to move here from Arizona a month ago. Just as it had egged him on from Georgia to Arizona. Always looking for something new. Something fun.

There was no one here to help her.

Melissa's eyes were drawn to the door of her room as it slowly opened. The first thing she saw was a big bouquet of carnations. The second thing was Del.

Chapter Three

Eight hours ago, when his shift had started, Del had intended to do nothing more complicated after work than go home, turn on the air-conditioning system and maybe, just maybe, if strength permitted, turn on the TV and catch the tail end of a Dodgers baseball game. The plan had had definite appeal.

But his plans had been disintegrated by the whimsical hand of fate that had put him in the right place at the right time. At Melissa's side.

So, instead of getting into his six-year-old flaming-red sports car and heading toward home when his shift was over, Del had showered at the precinct, changed into his civilian clothes and gone to the florist. When he walked into the store, he had no idea what he was going to get, just something bright and cheery. And then he had passed the display of carnations. They made him think of her—fragile, yet lasting, with a scent that clung to his skin. He had cleaned the store out of every pink-and-white carnation they had. Talking nonstop, the jovial woman behind the counter had artfully arranged the twenty-three flowers into a large white vase, finishing off her creation with a huge pink bow.

It sat next to him in the car as he drove to the hospital, strapped in with a seat belt on the passenger side. He wondered if perhaps it was a little too much. He wondered if it was enough. But mainly he wondered if she'd be pleased to see him again.

She was sitting up in bed when he walked in. There was no one else in the room. Maybe he wouldn't have noticed if there had been.

He hadn't remembered her looking this attractive before. Something that felt like a fist tightened in his stomach at the same time that he reminded himself that she was married. Her dark hair was brushed and fell in wavy rivers past her shoulders. Her features were fine and delicate and made him think of someone who could be found at a debutante party, despite the light blue-and-white hospital gown she wore. This wasn't someone a man would abandon.

Not a man in his right mind at any rate.

Her deep brown eyes opened wide in surprise when she saw him balancing the bouquet as he walked in. Something twisted inside of him, hot and pulsating. For the first time in his life, Del felt tongue-tied. His palms were damp against the glass, and the vase nearly slipped from his hands. His grip tightened just in time. But even though he came forward, he made no move to place the vase on her table or give the flowers to her. He was too busy just looking at her.

She knows you're staring. Say something, idiot. He gave a weak smile and said, "Hey, you look terrific."

Compliments made her uncomfortable. Her mother had always told her that compliments were meant to hide the truth, and only the vain actually believed them. "For a woman who just gave birth," she murmured self-consciously.

He glimpsed something in her eyes and wondered what it was. Discomfort?

"No, for anybody. Female, that is." He was tripping over his own tongue and it annoyed him. He *never* lost his cool. Until now.

His halting words made her smile. He was just trying to be nice, nothing more. She shrugged carelessly. "The nurse thought I could do with a little color. She brought me some makeup."

The woman, a grandmother eight times over, had insisted that Melissa would feel better if she put it on. Plunking the cosmetics down on the small table, the nurse had said. "This'll perk you up. Someone as pretty as you shouldn't be so sad eyed."

Melissa had started to protest. She had absolutely no interest in putting makeup on. She knew that no amount of powder and paint could possibly have any effect on the way she felt. But the warmhearted nurse had been persistent, so Melissa had gone along with it.

It wasn't the makeup, Del judged. He really hadn't looked at her that closely before. There hadn't been time. They'd had an emergency on their hands. And she had been frightened and worn. All that had distorted the image she had projected. But now that he looked, really looked, he felt a very definite physical pull that both distressed him and at the same time honed his interest. There was still that sadness in her eyes, but it only served to make her that much more alluring.

She was married, he reminded himself, as if to break the spell.

Damn.

He realized that she was looking at something he was holding. He looked down. Flowers. He was still standing there, holding them. *Nice going, Mr. Suave.* He thrust them toward her. "These are for you."

Carnations. She'd always loved carnations, ever since she had been a young girl and one year her mother had planted them in her garden. Alan had promised her carnations for her wedding day. Her eyes turned bright with tears. She blinked, trying not to think of that.

Melissa cleared her throat, pushing the lump away. She forced a smile. "I kind of figured that." She licked her lower lip nervously.

"I'll just put them here." Bracing the vase against his chest, he moved her table closer. The bouquet almost blotted her out. Looking around, he decided that the shelf against the wall was a better place for it. She could still reach them if she wanted to, and they didn't block her view. "There, now you can have a souvenir of our get-together." He turned around and shoved his hands deep into his pockets. "The vase, I mean."

It was important to him that she remember him, even if she was someone else's wife. He didn't explore why, couldn't explore why at the moment. He just knew it was. That was probably the reason he had turned into such a blithering idiot, he thought.

She traced a rippled petal with her forefinger, then braced herself with her hands on the bed. Leaning forward, she inhaled the soft fragrance. "I already have a souvenir. The baby," she added when he looked at her, puzzled.

He wondered if there were awards given out for being stupid, and if he had already won first prize. "Oh, right, the baby. How is she?"

Melissa had fallen in love with the baby the first moment she had seen her. "Beautiful."

He had already stopped by to see the infant on his way to Melissa's room. "Like her mother." The words slipped out naturally. He saw Melissa stiffen at the compliment. But why? She must have received them before, with her looks. And he didn't mean anything by it.

No, he did. If he were being honest with himself, he did. He wanted to give her compliments, to let her know how beautiful he thought she was, even though it could go no further than that.

She saw the puzzled look in Del's eyes. She shouldn't have reacted that strongly. He was only trying to be friendly.

But she couldn't help herself. She no longer trusted

empty, flattering words. Her mother's warning rang in her ears. That had been her undoing. She had trusted, she had believed what she had been told, and now she was paying the price.

Alan had always been so quick to compliment her, and she had taken each one at face value. But the compliments had been all there was, just superficial words, without depth, without substance. Without a future.

She needed to get hold of herself. Her thoughts were bouncing around, running rampant. This poor, nice man would think she was a lump. She had to say something. "Would you like to see her?" She reached for the cord to ring the nurse.

"I already did."

Melissa dropped the cord. He wasn't interested. Why should he be? It was only another child to him. Men didn't care about things like that, about children. Her father had always been too busy to pay any attention to her. He'd said that it was enough that he worked to put food on the table. Until the day he stopped.

"Right." She sighed, suddenly very tired. "You helped deliver her."

He should be going, he thought. She needed her rest. But he wanted to look at her for just a while longer. "Yes, but I meant just now." He jerked a thumb vaguely behind him. "In the nursery."

She looked at him, surprised. "You stopped at the nursery?"

Why did she sound so amazed? It was only natural,

wasn't it? He and the baby had a special bond. "Sure. Why not?"

Melissa shook her head, still uncertain of his motives. "No reason, I just didn't think that you'd be interested, really."

Even when she had offered to have the baby brought in, it was only because she felt so restless around Del. It would have given them something to talk about, a focus for his attention. She didn't know why, but it made her nervous when he looked at her. It wasn't a bad nervous, just one that seemed to anticipate things. What, she had no idea. She had absolutely no reason to anticipate anything, she told herself. Yet she did.

"Not be interested in her?" he echoed. Was she serious? "How could someone not be interested in something that's so cute and innocent?"

Open mouth, insert foot up to the ankle, he thought, annoyed with himself as soon as he had uttered the words. Del didn't have to look at Melissa's face to know he'd made a major blunder, reminding her that the baby's father *hadn't* been interested.

He looked over his shoulder. "Maybe I should walk out and come in again. I'd like to start all over. I'm not usually this awkward or insensitive."

His obvious discomfort made her temporarily forget about her own. She smiled and shook her head. A corner of the hospital-supplied gown slipped, exposing a shoulder that was almost alabaster in color. She pulled the gown back into place, aware that he was watching her. It made her feel very, very female. "You've been nothing more than kind, Officer."

He sat on the corner of the bed, next to her feet. He tried not to think of the fact that her body was just inches from his, covered only with a thin hospital gown and a blanket. "After what we've been through, I think you can call me Del. Officer has that 'but-I-was-only-doing-the-speed-limit' ring about it."

She laughed and he thought that he had never heard a more melodic sound in his life. The tension that seemed to be vibrating between them softened a little. But it was still obvious that there was something there between them, something that made them feel uncomfortable. Yet neither wanted this encounter to end.

"All right." She nodded. "Del."

He liked the way his name sounded on her tongue. It did him no good to remind himself, again, that she was married. This was all completely innocent, he staunchly maintained, knowing that he was lying.

Baby, think baby. It was safer. At least, for him. "Do you have a name for the baby?"

"Della." Her smile was shy as it took hold of the corners of her mouth.

It was incredible how touched he could be by an act seemingly so simple. People had children named after them every day. But not him. Not even his brother and sister had seen fit to give his name to any of their children. "You named the baby after me?"

She saw how pleased he was, and it made her doubly glad that she had chosen his name. "I thought it was only right. After all, if you hadn't been there when you were, I don't know what I would have done.''

She had the most incredible eyes, he thought. Dark brown, like semisweet chocolate. Semisweet chocolate had always been his weakness. "Why were you driving yourself to the hospital?"

She stiffened again involuntarily. She didn't want to think about that, about what had happened before, and what was to come after. She wanted to seek shelter in right now, in this moment, with her baby being taken care of and a roof over both their heads. "Because there wasn't anyone else to ask."

She looked uncomfortable again, but he had to ask. "No one?"

She picked at the bedclothes, avoiding his eyes. "No one."

He couldn't believe that. "As in everyone was busy?" There must have been someone, a neighbor, a friend she could have asked. What kind of people did she know?

Melissa raised her chin. She had to stop hiding from issues if she was going to take control of her life again. There was no *if*. She *had* to take control. She was all Della had left.

"As in there was no 'everybody.' We're—I'm—" she corrected herself; she was going to have to get used to using the singular again "—new here. I don't really know anyone."

He tried to imagine how terrible that had to be for her. He'd never been alone in his life, unless he had wanted to be. There was always someone around to turn to, even when he might not have wanted them around. "Who's going to help you with the baby when you go home?"

Home. Who says I've got a home to go to? "Me." She realized she said the word too sharply. An apologetic smile flittered across her lips. "If I still have somewhere to go when I leave here."

The awkward feeling disappeared, like a new, itchy sweater that he cast off and forgot. He leaned forward, equally stunned and appalled as her words sank in. "You don't have a home?"

Melissa shook her head and wished he wouldn't look at her like that. If he didn't stop, she was going to cry any second now. She didn't want his sympathy. She wanted strength from somewhere, strength to get through this and win. "I'm staying at a motel. We were supposed to get—to move yesterday."

She had almost said get married, but she had caught herself just in time. Shame had stopped her. There was no need for him to know she wasn't married. She didn't want him looking at her in that way people had when they suddenly thought you were less of a person. Or deserving of their pity.

"Tell me more about your husband," Del coaxed her softly. Without realizing it, he had slipped his hand over hers.

Although he might not have realized it, she did. For a brief moment, she sought comfort from it, but knew it was wrong. "Are you asking officially?"

Del looked down at his hand. The room felt pleasantly warm, yet her hand was cold beneath his. He looked up into her eyes. "I'm asking as a friend."

"A friend?" she echoed as if the word was utterly foreign to her. It'd been a long time since she had had a friend to confide in. They'd moved around so much in the past year, it had been hard for her to get to know anyone. Not for Alan, though. It was easy for him to strike up casual friendships in bars. Melissa had always stayed at home, wherever home was at the time.

He wanted to be her friend. He wanted more than that, but he'd settle for friend. "Yes, I think you could use one about now, from what you've told me." He felt her clench her hand beneath his, withdrawing.

"Friends know when not to ask questions."

"Not always."

Her gaze challenged his. "How about when they're asked not to?"

The first rule in a confrontation was to know when you could go forward and when to retreat. Del shrugged and retreated. "Then, yes."

For now. But the topic wasn't closed. He needed answers and he'd get them eventually.

It occurred to him that he was making plans that went beyond this evening's visit. Way beyond. Later he'd explore the ramifications of his line of thinking. Right now there were other things to concern him.

"So tell me, where *are* you planning to go with my namesake once you leave here?" He tried to sound casual, but wasn't certain if he had succeeded.

Did she have family somewhere who could help?

He found himself hoping that they were somewhere nearby, but the soft, southern lilt in her voice told him no. She'd be leaving the state. He found that that bothered him more than it should have.

"Where?" she echoed.

It was the question that had been bouncing about in her head ever since she had arrived in the hospital. She couldn't stay here long. The insurance policy only covered two days. Thank God that even though Della was slightly premature she was well and healthy enough to leave with her. Even her short nap hadn't blocked out her concern. It had appeared in her dream. She was lost, running from path to path, searching for a way out of a maze. Except there hadn't been one.

She saw that he was waiting for an answer. "Well, first back to the motel to get my things." The only thing that Alan had left behind besides the van was her suitcase of clothes. And the record collection she had insisted on taking with them. It was all she had of her childhood. She'd spent hours listening to those worn forty-fives. Hopefully, the motel manager hadn't confiscated them.

No, she consoled herself, there was no reason to do that yet. The room was paid for until the end of the week. She had seen to that herself.

"And then?" Del prompted gently, instinctively knowing that if he pressed too hard, he might frighten her into silence.

I don't know, she thought impatiently. "You're asking questions again."

He pretended not to notice the edge in her voice. "It's kind of hard talking to someone you just met without questions."

Despite herself, Melissa smiled. He had a way of twisting a sentence, turning it to his advantage. Two could play at that game. "I thought I was a friend, not a stranger."

"Friendships grow stronger the more you know about each other." He thought he had her there.

"Not always." She looked off. "Sometimes familiarity breeds contempt."

The look on her face haunted him. "Is that what happened?" He'd blurted out the question automatically, without thinking.

She looked at him sharply. *Please, please, leave it alone.* "I thought I said—"

"Sorry." Del held up his hands before she could get any further. "I thought I could sneak one in there." He grinned at her sheepishly.

His manner totally disarmed her. "You probably make a good policeman."

"I make a great one," he said without conceit, "but we're not talking about me."

"We're not talking about me, either." She raised her knees up to her chest and folded her arms around them. "Please?"

She needed space, and he was too eager to learn. For now he would back away before he frightened her off altogether. But it wasn't easy. He'd never been one to plod along slowly. He'd always been the one to take the ball and run. "Think the Angels have a chance at the pennant?"

Melissa rested her head on her arms and started to laugh. "I haven't the slightest idea."

He liked making her laugh. He decided that she had had much too little laughter in her life of late. He leaned forward. "Want to know about me?"

Melissa raised her head. She began to say no, but realized that she did. Besides, if he talked about himself, he couldn't ask her questions. She took a deep breath and sat up. "All right. Tell me about you."

"I come from an average-size Italian family. Five boys, one girl. Kathleen always felt put upon."

Melissa tried to envision that and found herself yearning. "Was she?" From where she sat, having brothers to tease her, to care for and be cared about, sounded wonderful.

"Sure." He shrugged, not giving it much thought. "She was our sister. That was her job." And they were always there for each other, when it counted.

He saw Melissa's obvious interest and went on more rapidly. "I rode my first motorcycle at six."

"Six?" she scoffed. "Nobody lets a six-year-old ride a motorcycle." Even her mother would have said something about that, and she hadn't really cared. No, it was when she was eight that her mother had stopped caring, stopped living. The year her father left.

"That's what my mother yelled at my Uncle Joe. It was his motorcycle. He took me for a ride down Pacific Coast Highway. The beach to my left, the open road whizzing by in front of me. It was fantastic." He grinned at her. "From then on, I was hooked."

"Is that why you became a motorcycle cop?"

To her surprise, he admitted it. "Yes. That was the only career that would let me ride a motorcycle and still be respectable enough to suit Ma."

She studied his face more closely. If someone had asked, she would have guessed that he was a free soul who didn't much care about anyone's opinion. That he cared what his mother thought of him gave him another dimension. "Is that important?"

"What?" He had never thought a hospital gown was sexy, until now. Hers kept slipping first from one shoulder, then the other as she adjusted it. It made him lose his train of thought.

"Is it important to please your mother?"

"Yes," he replied without hesitation. Though there were times when she could be a nuisance, he loved his mother dearly and freely admitted it. He had always regarded Gina Santini as one hell of a lady.

Melissa liked that, liked the fact that he wasn't ashamed of expressing his feelings for his mother. "I hope my daughter feels that way about me someday."

How could anyone help but love her? he thought. Then he remembered her husband. "If not, send her to me, I'll straighten her out." He winked.

It was an exceedingly sexy wink. Only a dead person would have been immune to it, she thought, trying to explain why, after having given birth less than half a day ago, she was feeling a flutter in her stomach at such a harmless physical action.

"I have no idea where I'll be. Then, or now," she added in a whisper.

When she raised her eyes again, she saw that he was watching her. A horrible wave of loneliness washed over her. She had no idea whether it was because of her hormones running amok after having been thrown out of kilter by the birth process, or if her emotional equilibrium had been thrown completely off by Alan's disappearance.

Whatever it was, she felt very, very vulnerable right now. She had thought she didn't want sympathy, and maybe she wouldn't again in a little while. But right at this moment, she was in desperate need of someone with sympathetic deep blue eyes. Del's were cobalt blue and seemed to coax words out of her even when she wanted to keep them locked up tight inside.

"I have no money and nowhere to go." She licked her lips, trying to save face. But it was too late for that and she knew it. "You're a policeman. Maybe you could tell me where I could apply for—" the words burned on her tongue but she had to think of Della "—for aid."

If he ever got his hands on that bastard who deserted her—

Del reined himself in. Threats he couldn't carry out wouldn't do her any good. Offhand, he couldn't remember the names of the agencies that could help her. Kathleen would know things like that. She was forever into community good works. He'd ask her.

But whatever Kathleen had to tell him, he had a sneaking suspicion that it really wouldn't make a difference in the long run. The die had been cast. "I could look into it," he told her, "and get back to you tomorrow."

Melissa kept her smile fixed on her face. He wouldn't be back tomorrow. Why should he? What was she to him? She still didn't really understand why he had returned tonight, although she had been very glad he had. There was something incredibly comforting about having him here, like a warm fire after a tramp through the first winter snow. "Fine. Tomorrow."

He heard it in her voice, saw it in her eyes. She was distancing herself again. She didn't believe him.

Well, why the hell should she? She'd undoubtedly believed her husband when he had vowed to love, honor and obey, and he had apparently vanished from the face of the earth the first opportunity he got.

No, he wasn't being fair about this, Del thought. He didn't know the details that were involved in the case. Maybe there were extenuating circumstances.

And then he looked at Melissa's face. He didn't have to know the details. No extenuating circumstances on earth would have made him leave her if he'd been in the other man's place.

That was when Del knew what he was going to do.

"Tomorrow," he repeated.

Chapter Four

Del knew that there were a dozen different reasons, if not more, against what he proposed to do. And they all had to do with common sense, something Gina Santini had tried to instill in all her children over the years. But she had also instilled them with a great capacity for compassion and understanding. She had taught them to put themselves in someone else's position and see things through their eyes. When Del looked through Melissa's eyes, when he looked *into* Melissa's eyes, his reaction was one that couldn't be smothered by logic.

He knew exactly what he wanted to do. What he had to do.

Still, in deference to common sense, Del said nothing to Melissa about his idea. That gave him a little more than half a day to think about it carefully. To let his impulse cool.

He'd finally left Melissa's room when the night-duty nurse had peeked in and sympathetically but firmly informed him that visiting hours had been over for more than half an hour.

Though she hadn't said anything more than "Thank you for coming," the look in Melissa's eyes told Del that she was sorry to see him go. The stack against common sense began to grow higher.

He lay awake half that night, dutifully listing the pros and cons of the situation in his mind. By the end of his shift the next day, he had gone over all the reasons against his decision five or six times. Each time he did, they all rang very true, very logical.

And didn't mean a damn thing to him. He was going with "pro." He'd always meant to.

At bottom, he had always gone with impulse, with gut feelings. And for the most part, it had turned out all right. He vividly remembered Sister Mary Margaret, the seventh-grade nun he had had who was so tall she could have played center on a basketball team, solemnly shaking her head during a parent-teacher conference with his mother. She had told Gina Santini that unlike her first born, Nicholas, Delveccio had all the earmarks of a boy bound for hell on a toboggan. His path was paved with impulses.

"I'm not going there yet, Sister," he muttered to himself under his breath as he walked into the larger of the two toy stores at the mall and pointed out the teddy bear in the window. The teddy bear that took up *most* of the window. He felt that if he was going to do things, it was going to be in a big way.

Maybe then she wouldn't say no.

* * *

Melissa kept watching the door. Every sound, every movement, had her raising her eyes, waiting to see the door open. When it did, it was always someone else walking in, a nurse, an orderly, the doctor the hospital had assigned to her.

Never Del.

She sighed, upbraiding herself for being such a hopeless idiot, even as she looked at the clock again. Eleven minutes since the last time she'd looked.

There was absolutely no reason to believe that the man was going to return to the hospital just to see her, even though he had said he would. That had only been polite conversation on his part, as in "see you around," she told herself, wadding the bedclothes on both sides of her.

Annoyed with herself, Melissa smoothed the light blanket out, then restlessly shifted. She'd gone on several walks down the hallway today, moving a lot slower than she was happy about. Each time her destination had been the nursery. She had stood, watching her daughter sleep, while she gathered her energy for the trip back. She was determined to build up her strength. She'd need it after today.

The door opened and she caught her breath. But it was her nurse with Della. "Someone here to see you," the woman said cheerfully, placing the baby in Melissa's arms.

She was surprised at the visit. "Is she hungry again?" Melissa asked.

The dark woman beamed. "Honey, they're always hungry at this stage. But right now, I thought you might want a little bonding with her while she's not wailing."

"She cries a lot?" Each time that they'd brought Della in, the baby had either been on the verge of falling asleep, or sleeping.

"Best lungs in the nursery." The nurse laughed, patting Melissa's arm. "I'll be back in a little while," she promised. The door swung closed behind her. Melissa stared at it.

Why had he said he'd come back when he wasn't planning to?

Melissa bit her lower lip. *Grow up, for heaven's sake. Everybody says things they don't mean. Everybody.*

He was nothing to her and she nothing to him. They had shared nature's most wondrous event, but the afterglow of that had surely faded for him by now and he was getting on with his life.

As she would with hers.

"He's not going to come here, and Mommy's a fool for thinking that he might," she told the very tiny bundle in her arms. Della only looked at her with sleepy blue eyes. "But then, Mommy's getting rather good at that."

Gently she placed her cheek against her daughter's and felt a wave of comfort wash over her. This, this little person in her arms, was to be her reality and nothing else. She had a child to take care of and a life to put together for them any way she knew how.

She held Della against her breast again. The baby was asleep. She would take the first steps to getting them a good life once they left the shelter of these walls, Melissa promised herself.

Maybe the motel manager had a heart. Maybe he would let them stay there a few weeks until she could find a job and pay him back. She thought of the thick-featured man. And then again, maybe not.

If not, there had to be some place she could apply for temporary aid. All she needed was a little time to get back on her feet. A little time to get her life into gear. After all, she had an education. She had the determination. She had— A giant white teddy bear entering her room.

Melissa sat up a little straighter, surprised. "Del?" she whispered.

Uncertainty and hope rang in the single word, and he heard both. Still holding the three-foot-high fuzzy bear in front of him, Del peered around the stuffed animal's body. "You guessed."

She wanted to laugh, to cry. To hug him. She settled for transferring her emotions to Della. It was a lot safer that way. But she did smile. Broadly. "What is that thing?"

Del lifted the toy he was holding toward her. "You can't tell?"

"Yes, but—" Melissa looked at the sleeping baby in her arms. "Santini, babies need teddy bears you can stick into a crib. That one is at least five times as big as she is." Melissa used his surname in an effort to cloak her emotions. Still, she was filled with affection for him. It was a terribly sweet thing to do.

He was undaunted. "She'll grow into it. It'll give her a goal."

He propped the unwieldy bear on the blue vinyl chair by the window and came forward to look at Della. Babies, all the fathers at the precinct had solemnly testified, were ugly at this stage. That was just the way it was. Their faces were flattened, with reddish blotches here and there, their heads misshapen. Trolls in miniature bodies. Faces only mothers could love. He'd heard it over and over, and had even gotten to believe it, the way he did when the weatherman told him about the temperature.

Moving the blanket slowly aside so he could see her better, Del looked down into Della's face. There was no doubt about it. With a fringe of black hair, a perfectly round face and proportioned features, she was absolutely beautiful. A tiny rosebud waiting to unfold.

Something stirred within him—love, pride. Joy. He smiled as he lightly swept a finger along her tightly clenched fist. "Hi, kid," he whispered softly. "Remember me?"

Della shifted a little in response to his voice. She opened her eyes for a moment and actually seemed to be looking at him. But then she closed them again.

"I think she does," Melissa said, trying not to notice how much this small scene was affecting her. She couldn't get caught up in it, in him. She couldn't board another roller coaster, especially when she felt so emotionally needy.

Del looked up from the infant and grinned. "A lady always remembers the first guy who held her." He settled back comfortably on the far corner of the bed, just as he had done yesterday.

A comforting feeling of déjà vu washed over Melissa. For the moment, she'd let herself savor the contentment his presence generated. As long as she remembered that all this was just temporary, she'd be all right. Her mistake was always in believing that good things would last.

"You're an expert, I take it?" There must have been plenty of first ladies in his life, she would imagine. A man as darkly handsome as he was certainly wouldn't lack for constant companionship.

The sexy look was back in his eyes as he innocently said, "I read a lot."

Though something pulled inside her, she didn't allow herself to get lost in that gaze. "Speaking of reading, did you have a chance to, um—" God, how she hated asking favors, even one that wasn't only for her. It wasn't in her nature to accept, only to give. Sitting on the other side of the table, on the receiving end, made her miserably uncomfortable.

He read her mood in her eyes. "Look into your problem?" he guessed.

Problem. It was far more than that. "Yes."

There would be no turning back once he said it. "I did and I have."

She couldn't shake the feeling that she was allowing herself to be reduced to a supplicant, a number on a dole. It went against everything she had ever hoped for, everything she'd ever believed in. Her words felt like lead in her mouth. She held the baby closer, as if shielding her from the degradation she felt. "You found an agency for me to apply to."

He shook his head. "Not exactly."

Her eyes narrowed. He'd confused her. "What, then, exactly?"

"It's kind of like a benevolent policemen's society." He saw her frown deepen. Del picked up speed. "Actually, it only involves one benevolent policeman." He took a breath.

"You?" she guessed.

"Me."

"What?" Only the baby in her arms kept her from shouting the question. He had to be crazy.

He couldn't tell if it was shocked surprise in her voice or angry astonishment. He tried to sound as reassuring as possible. "You can stay with me until you get back on your feet."

Did he think that just because she was down on her luck, she could be had so easily?

Anger at the suggestion warred with the sight of the teddy bear sitting on the chair, seemingly looking out the window. A man who could think of a baby when he didn't have to couldn't be an opportunistic creep. At least, not completely.

She looked at his face. No, he wasn't a creep, just misdirected.

Melissa shook her head. "I don't think so."

It was what he was afraid of. She thought he wanted to take advantage of her. "It's not what you think."

Her expression was wary. "It's not?"

The way she looked at him had Del uncertain again. She was the only woman he had ever known he couldn't second-guess. "That is, well, I don't know what you think." His voice had Della stirring and making noises. He lowered it quickly, leaning forward as he all but whispered, "But there's nothing improper about this."

His face was inches away from hers. His lips were inches from hers. Melissa felt a shiver travel up her spine. She moved back in self-defense, suddenly afraid of what she was feeling. "You do this all the time, Santini?"

"No," he admitted with a shrug, trying to seem casual and hide his growing frustration.

Damn it, she needed a place to stay. Why was she fighting him on this? He was honorable. He couldn't help the thoughts he was having about her, but she wasn't a mind reader.

"But I never delivered a baby before, either. This is a special situation," he insisted. "I have a house," he added hurriedly, seeing that she was weakening. "Actually, it was my brother's and mine, but Drew moved out last year to get married and I bought out his half."

"Policemen make that much money?" she asked suspiciously, wondering if she was making another mistake believing him.

"I'm good for it. I make monthly payments. Some people trust me."

She could see how they would. She did. Not completely, of course, she could never trust again completely, but just enough to believe that his offer was genuine, without any hidden motives.

But she still felt exceedingly hesitant. There was pride in the way. "I'd rather go to an agency." She didn't want to offend him. "It's impersonal—"

"Do you want impersonal?" He looked at Della pointedly before looking at Melissa again. "Remember, we're friends."

It was a lovely term that really didn't apply, not that she didn't want it to. "You don't know me—"

And whose fault is that? Melissa thought, breaking off her sentence.

"Not 'cause I haven't tried. I think," he went on easily, feeling a little more confident of the outcome, "you're the most closemouthed woman I've ever met. But then, I figure the baby'll make up for the silence once she gets going." He wanted to hold Della, to feel the tiny life in his arms again, but first he had to convince Melissa that he was right.

She was tempted. But she was afraid of the things that might happen. Of the way he made her feel. "I can't—"

He looked at her calmly. Didn't she see there were no other options really available to her? "Why not? You don't have anywhere else to go and no money to go with, you said so yourself."

"I won't accept charity." Melissa set her jaw stubbornly.

There it was, he thought. Her pride. While pride was a good sign, showing that she hadn't given up, he couldn't let that get in the way of her welfare, neither hers nor Della's. "You were willing to accept it from an agency," he pointed out. "Besides, who said anything about charity? We'll work something out."

That was part of what she was worried about. She arched one brow as she pinned him with a look. "Exactly what did you have in mind?"

Lots of things, none of which I'm at liberty to disclose. "I'll charge you rent," he said, knowing he was gaining ground. "You can repay me when you get back on your feet."

She didn't understand him. Men like him didn't exist. They were part of her imagination, not the real world. Hadn't she found that out?

"Why are you doing this?" She felt if she looked into his eyes, she'd see the truth. If he was lying to her, she'd know. She saw a lot of things there, none of which she could begin to understand. Or let herself try to.

He grew serious. "Because I don't want my namesake out in the street." He placed his hand lightly on her arm. "I don't want her spending her first days at some mission where the roaches are all bigger than she is."

Melissa's eyes grew large. She looked down at the

infant in her arms. She hadn't thought about that. "Is it really like that?"

"Have I scared you?"

"Yes."

"Then it's like that." He'd fight dirty if he had to. Del raised his hand in a mock pledge. "Scout's honor, you've got nothing to fear from me, if that's what's stopping you. I'll give you my mother's phone number. You can call her if I misbehave."

She laughed and Della woke up, silently looking at the two people around her. He raised his brow in a question as he reached for the infant. Melissa nodded and handed Della to him. She watched in fascination as he cradled the tiny soul to him. He did it with such ease. "You really are unique."

His finger inside the tiny hand, he looked up at Melissa. "Does that mean we have a deal?"

Melissa shivered, whether from the cold or from anticipation, she wasn't certain. "I guess I have no choice."

He kept his eyes on Melissa. He'd make her smile again, he promised himself. "Not much, at any rate."

They shook hands on it.

Melissa looked at the clock in her room. The minute hand was four strokes shy of the twelve, the hour hand was touching the three. She had told Del that the doctor was discharging her at three o'clock. If she wasn't on her way out by then, she'd be charged for another full day. And her policy wouldn't cover it. It was something called patient convenience.

Something she no longer had, she thought. Nothing was convenient anymore.

She tried not to think about it as she changed Della, tucking around her the tiny diaper that the hospital had supplied. The nurse on duty had brought the baby in twenty minutes ago, wheeling her in the clear bassinet. Both she and Della were almost ready.

And Del wasn't here.

She should have known.

Melissa tucked the blanket around Della the way the nurse had shown her. Only one arm and a tiny face peered out.

"Makes 'em feel safe and secure," the woman had told her. Well, at least one of them could feel that way, Melissa thought, pinning the loose end.

"He's thought it over, honey," she said to Della, "and decided that he was making promises he couldn't keep."

She paused, taking a deep breath. She was going to be fine, just fine. She'd been alone before. Now they'd be alone together, she and Della. She looked down at the bassinet. "Remember that. Don't believe anyone. Except me."

Because she needed the contact, Melissa lifted the baby into her arms. "I'll never lie to you."

She sighed, moving toward the window. The sky was hazy today, and she could hardly see the sailboats on the ocean. But she knew they were there, just temporarily hidden from view. Like the solutions to her problems.

"It's just you and me, honey. But we'll make it. Somehow, someway, we're going to make it."

Although at the moment she hadn't the slightest idea how.

"Is someone picking you up?" Melissa whirled around to see the nurse entering again. She was pushing a wheelchair in front of her.

"No, I—" Melissa frowned at the wheelchair. "What's that for?"

"Hospital policy." The woman patted the seat. "We have to wheel you out. We can't take a chance on you hurting yourself while you're with us. You're still weak, you know."

In more ways than one, Melissa thought.

"If no one's coming for you, we can call you a cab," the nurse offered. It was evident to Melissa from her voice that the woman didn't approve of the fact that no one was coming for her.

Melissa shook her head. There was no money for a cab. Besides, her car was still in the hospital parking lot. Del had told her so. "No, my car's in the lot. I'll be fine. Really," she added when the nurse's frown grew deeper.

"This is highly unusual—"

"So's the rest of my life." Melissa tried to smile, but the effort hurt too much. With this latest disappointment, she was out of reasons to smile.

Turning, she sank into the wheelchair, still holding tightly on to Della. "Just wheel me to your front entrance, so that everything's done properly, and I'll take it from there."

The nurse didn't like the situation one bit. She looked at the door, as if willing someone to appear for the young woman in the room. "Wait, I'll have to get someone to bring a cart for your flowers."

Her carnations. The flowers that he had brought to her. "Leave the flowers." She didn't want to be reminded of her latest disappointment. Her latest stupidity.

The nurse didn't move. "How about the teddy bear?" She gestured toward the huge white bear. It was still sitting where Del had put it yesterday.

Melissa was about to tell her to forget about the bear as well, but then stopped. The bear wasn't hers. It was Della's. It would probably be a long while before she could afford to buy Della any toys to play with. "I'll take the bear."

The nurse looked at the stuffed animal uncertainly. "I suppose I could manage with that and still push your chair to the elevator."

"That's okay," a voice behind them called out. "I'll carry the bear. And the flowers."

Melissa turned to see Del hurrying into the room, still in uniform. He looked as if he had run up the stairs, all six flights, rather than wait for the elevator.

Which was exactly what he had done.

He scooped up the bear under one arm, the flower arrangement resting precariously under his other. "Sorry. There was a robbery just as I was getting off duty. The guy didn't have the good grace to do it half an hour later when I wasn't around."

He saw the look of relief on Melissa's face. It

stopped him dead in his tracks. "Did you think I wasn't coming?"

"No, I just thought..." Her voice trailed off.

She was lying. She hadn't thought he was returning. She didn't trust him yet. Progress was going to be a lot slower than he thought. But they'd work on it. He curbed his disappointment, telling himself it was too soon for her.

He looked around the room, sparing her from coming up with an excuse. "Nothing else?"

"I didn't come with anything else," she reminded him. "Except my purse." She pointed toward it on her bed. "And that bag the hospital's giving me for the baby."

A new-mother care package, the nurse had called it. Filled with a little bit of everything a new mother needed before her husband ran off to the store to buy supplies in earnest.

If there was a husband, Melissa thought ruefully.

Del set down the bear and tried to figure out a way to juggle everything in one trip.

"I'll get that cart," the nurse said in a no-nonsense voice. But she was wearing a wide smile as she left.

Logistics suddenly occurred to Melissa. "What about my van?" He couldn't drive both his car and hers.

"I already took care of that." He placed the flowers on the table as he waited. "I had one of the other guys drop me off in the hospital parking lot before my shift this morning. I drove your van to my house."

"But I have the keys." She looked down at her purse.

He grinned. Her innocence charmed him. "There're certain things you pick up along the way."

"As a policeman?" she guessed.

"As a teenager. I drove my mother's car when I was fifteen." He grinned, remembering. "It wasn't exactly with her permission."

She shook her head. "You really must have been something else when you were growing up." A regular hellion, probably. When had he learned to be so nice?

"So my mother likes to tell me. She says that all her gray hairs are named Del."

"I thought you said you had brothers and a sister."

"Four altar boys and a would-be saint. Not a lick of trouble from the whole lot." He grinned again. "Except for me."

She could believe it. There was a streak of mischief in his eyes. "You must have been an interesting change."

He heard the cart squeaking in the hall as it approached. "Not to hear Ma talk about it. Ah, she's back." He took the cart from the nurse and deposited the flower arrangement, the teddy bear and Melissa's care package onto it. Gripping the cart's handle, he turned to the nurse. "Ready to roll when you are."

"Not everybody gets a police escort when they leave the hospital," the nurse chuckled as she brought

Melissa's wheelchair up to the passenger side of Del's black-and-white squad car.

Melissa looked at the car. "I thought you drove a motorcycle." Holding on to the sides of the car, Melissa eased herself into the seat, hating the fact that she was still so stiff. She had visions of springing back by now. This was definitely not springing. Buckled in, she held her arms out, waiting for the nurse to place her daughter in them.

"I couldn't see bringing you and Della home on the back of a bike. I swapped with Larry as I was leaving the burglary. Told him I had to pick you up."

"Larry?" The name was vaguely familiar, but she couldn't put a face to it.

"The policeman who drove us to the hospital the other day. He was at the robbery site, too." Del laughed. "I would have liked to have been there when he climbed on my motorcycle and started it up." Larry definitely did not have the build for a motorcycle.

The nurse closed the door for Melissa, then leaned over, looking in through the open window. "Well, I wish you and your wife all the luck in the world, Officer."

"Thanks."

Melissa opened her mouth, but Del pulled away from the curb before she had a chance to correct the nurse.

Chapter Five

"This is where you live?"

Del looked around the small, dingy motel room. It felt cramped, even though there was hardly anything in it. The faded yellow paint was peeling, the bargain-store cast-off furniture, what there was of it, was old and dilapidated. There was a stale, musty odor hanging over the room, and when he had tried to close the door behind them, Del noticed that the lock had been jimmied open recently. It offered absolutely no protection whatsoever. He was glad she was getting out of here.

He had tried to keep the distaste from his voice, but Melissa had detected it. There was no use in trying to hide behind empty pride, not in this case. She handed Della to him and pulled her battered suitcase out from under the bed.

She shrugged as she placed it on the faded orange-

and-white fringed bedspread. "It was all we could afford. We were running low on funds." Her funds, she thought. God, what a fool she had been.

He watched her as she opened the narrow closet. There wasn't much there to take out. "What is it that your husband does?"

She turned, about to tell him that she and Alan hadn't been married. She hated lies, even little ones, but something stopped her from telling Del the truth. A small kernel of self-preservation. If Del believed she was married, there would be no danger of any sort of entanglement between them. She needed that assurance, more for herself than because of him. She'd made too many mistakes already. This would keep her from making another.

Melissa turned back to the closet and took an armload of clothes out. "Not much of anything, lately."

There was more, he could have sworn to it. There was something in her eyes that told him she was holding back, something she wanted to tell him but didn't. He shifted Della to the right, his arm growing stiff. "What made you marry him?" He watched a small, sad smile slip across her lips.

"Dreams, mostly." Her laugh was short and self-deprecating. She'd been stupid. And hopeful. "I bought into the happily-ever-after syndrome." She looked at him. "Pretty silly, I guess, in this day and age."

He would have willingly wrapped his hands around her husband's throat for doing this to her. "I hear romance and all that good stuff are making a comeback." Della started to whimper, and he jiggled her a little. Soothed by the rocking motion, Della settled down again.

He was good with her, Melissa thought. Too bad he wasn't Della's father instead of the one Della had. The one she would never know.

Melissa snapped her suitcase shut. "Can't tell by me." She sighed. "That's it."

He stared. He'd packed three himself on his last vacation. "One suitcase?"

"And that one." She pointed to a sturdier-looking one that stood off in the corner. "I travel light."

Carefully he handed Della back to Melissa and took her suitcase off the bed. "A very good attribute."

Somehow he had managed to coax a smile out of her. He kept doing that, she thought. "You're determined to be cheerful about this, aren't you?"

"One of my failings." He crossed to the other suitcase and grabbed the handle. Expecting more clothes, he was surprised at its weight. When he had to strain to lift it, he looked at Melissa quizzically. "What do you have in here, rocks?"

"Records." He saw a fond look cross her face when she told him. "Forty-fives," she clarified. "All my favorite songs."

Bracing himself, he hefted the suitcase up, then moved toward her. "Have a lot of them, don't you?"

"It's hard to choose." She could never bear to leave even one behind. That would have been like throwing out an old friend.

"C'mon." With a suitcase in each hand, listing to

one side, Del nodded toward the door. "Let's blow this two-bit place," he joked.

She opened the door for him and walked out first. Now that she was outside, she was really glad to leave this place and its memories behind.

She held Della closer as she walked down the open stairway in front of Del. "They didn't charge two bits." She'd been surprised at how much the rooms did rent for. Things were so much cheaper back home. But Alan hadn't wanted to go back. Only forward. It was as if he'd been running from something. She realized now it was commitment.

Del placed the suitcases on the ground next to his car and opened the trunk. To his left, he saw someone watching him from behind a faded orange-and-white curtain. There was probably a lot going on here that couldn't bear up to the light of day. "Rent all paid up?"

"Until the end of the week. Today," she suddenly realized out loud.

He slammed the trunk down again, suitcases safely inside. "I always did have perfect timing."

There was a look in his eyes that she didn't know how to interpret, so she left it alone. "I'm—I'm really grateful for this, Del."

It cost her to say that, so he played it down. "No big deal."

Maybe not to him, but it was to her.

They dropped off the key with the grumpy-looking manager and drove away.

Melissa closed her eyes as The Merry Maid Motel

faded from view behind them, relieved to be on her way. She had hated it when they had arrived, but Alan had promised her that it was only a temporary stay, like all the others. She hadn't realized that this time he had meant temporary for him.

Bitterness stung her heart as she thought that the man she'd given her love to had been so willing to leave her in the dust without so much as a second thought while he went on with his life.

Slowing for a changing light, Del saw the solemn look on her face. "You sure you don't want me to try to find him for you?" It was a question that had to be asked, even though he didn't want to.

Della's whimper had begun to escalate in urgency. Melissa rocked her against her breast. "I'm sure. I never want to see him again as long as I live."

He grinned. "Good."

There was that look again. Melissa wondered if he was aware of it. He looked pleased that Alan was out of her life and that she didn't want him back. Or was that just her imagination? Was she just being over-wrought?

Probably overwrought, Melissa decided. There was that one stubborn streak within her that refused to stop hoping that something wonderful was waiting for her just around the corner. She should know by now that there never was.

Della began to cry in earnest. It was definitely, Del thought, the sort of plaintive wail that had a message attached to it. He glanced at Melissa as he took a turn to the right. "That either means that she's tired or wet or hungry." He considered the choices. "She just woke up, so she's not tired."

Melissa felt inside the blanket, testing the rim of the back of the diaper gingerly before venturing further. "And she's not wet."

Del nodded it. "Hungry has it."

What was she going to do about that in the car? Melissa wet her lips. "I'm breast-feeding her."

It was a perfectly natural thing. Mothers had done it since the beginning of time. Why in heaven's name did telling him make her feel she was imparting intimate information?

Del pulled the car over to the curb. With the engine still running, he pulled up the hand brake and threw the car into park. Melissa watched, curious, as he turned and reached for something in the back seat.

He'd put the hospital's care package there. Rummaging, he found a receiving blanket. It was smaller than the kind Kathleen had had, he remembered, but it would do. Turning around again, Del draped the white blanket with its cheery pink-and-blue sheep over Melissa's shoulder so that it completely covered her left breast.

"What are you doing?" She raised her voice above Della's wail to be heard.

"There you go." He grinned as he gestured toward the blanket. "Privacy."

She looked down and realized that he was right. With a minimum of effort, she could feed Della and no one would even notice. Melissa looked at Del, grateful that he understood when she couldn't even find the right words to explain her feelings. "You certainly think of everything."

All the thanks he needed was in her eyes. "Part Boy Scout, part supercop."

And all man.

The thought flashed across her mind from out of nowhere, unannounced, as if it had been lying in wait to ambush her when she least expected it. She was emotionally vulnerable and she knew it. Feelings of gratitude could mushroom into something far more potent. She had to be careful to lead with her head and not with her heart. She'd done that already and look where it had gotten her. Penniless, homeless, in a squad car with a newborn baby.

And a policeman up for the Sir Lancelot award of the decade.

Trying not to think of the fact that he was only inches away from her, Melissa carefully undid the top three buttons of her caftan. Turning Della around, she positioned the baby, trying not to notice that Del's knuckles had turned white as he gripped the steering wheel.

Within moments, Della was quiet as she greedily satisfied her hunger.

Melissa patted the baby's bottom gently as she nursed. "You really are very thoughtful, Del."

When she spoke softly like that, it got right under his skin. It was like feeling waves of beautiful music enveloping him, or like an evening spring breeze that caressed and soothed.

And made his fancy drift.

Except that drifting wasn't advisable here. And not just because he was pulling onto the Pacific Coast Highway, heading north into traffic. That was the easy part. The hard part was shutting out thoughts about the woman sitting next to him. It was much too soon to think of her as anything other than a person in need. He'd been trained to help. Raised to help people in need. That was all he should be thinking about right now.

But God, she was beautiful. He stole a glance, then looked back at the road. Her hair about her shoulders, a child at her breast, Melissa was a living portrait of a Madonna and child for some aspiring young artist to capture on canvas.

A car abruptly changed lanes in front of him and Del had to brake to keep from hitting it. Cursing himself, he strove to concentrate on driving and nothing else.

When Del pulled into his driveway fifteen minutes later, he was surprised to see Larry waiting there, leaning against the hood of his car. Del had left the sports car in the precinct parking lot.

Larry approached the passenger's side of the squad car as Del cut off the engine. "I thought I'd bring your car around and save you the trouble. Seeing as how you've got your hands full." He beamed at Melissa, nodded a greeting and leaned into the car as Del got out. "Mind if I take a look at the baby? I never got a chance to see her. They whisked you off so fast."

"Of course not." It pleased her to show Della off. Feeling to make sure that all her buttons were fastened again, Melissa pulled back the blanket. Della blinked against the hazy light.

"Face like an angel," Larry pronounced. "Well," he straightened, moving away from the car. "I guess I'd better be going."

Del took out the second suitcase, placing it next to the first. He tossed Larry the keys and went to help Melissa out of the car.

"You okay?" he asked, noting that the color in her face was fading.

She nodded, though she was beginning to feel wobbly.

"Here, don't forget this." Larry pulled the box from the hospital out of the back seat, followed by the flower arrangement and the huge teddy bear, depositing them all next to the suitcases. The bear sat in the driveway, guarding everything.

Positioning himself behind the steering wheel of his car, Larry threw the lever into reverse. He stuck his head out the window as he pulled away. "Give me a holler if you need anything."

"He's a nice man." She indicated the departing squad car.

"Yes, he is." Del unlocked the front door and guided her in. "Watch your step."

Melissa stared as she crossed the threshold. The living room looked as if two pit bulls had had an all-day tug-of-war on the premises. "You mean that literally, don't you?'' she called over her shoulder as he went to bring her suitcases in.

Everything from newspapers to dishes to shoes were scattered around the room and into the hall, left where they had been dropped the night before. Or the week before, from the looks of it.

"This is where you live?" she asked, echoing the words he had said to her less than half an hour ago.

"Doesn't it look it?" Stopping a minute, Del scooped up a shirt and a sock off the sofa, clearing a place for her. He dropped them on another chair, wondered where the mate to the sock was. It was one of the reasons he bought all his socks in one color.

"Yes." She drew out the word as she looked around. "It certainly does." She wondered how he could stand living like this. How did he ever manage to find anything in this clutter? She turned to him. "Um—"

He anticipated what he thought was her question. "Your room's back there, through the family room."

Suitcases in hand, he gestured with the lighter one toward the room he had set aside for her.

Unlike the rest of the house that they passed through, the guest room wasn't a mess, only dusty. He set down the suitcases, making a mental note to bring in the rest of the things from the driveway. "I don't get a chance to clean much," he explained, opening a window.

"Too busy riding to the rescue."

He turned and saw she was smiling at him. It shot shafts of warm desire through him. This was going to be some test of moral fortitude, he told himself, having her here. "Something like that."

She looked around. The room was a pale blue, with light gray drapes at the window, a comfortable double bed buffered by two nightstands. A matching bureau of honey-colored wood stood on the other side.

"It's very nice." It reminded her of the room she had had at Aunt Julia's house, where she stayed when her mother was too oblivious to the world to care for her. Except that this was much nicer, much newer-looking.

She stood for a moment, silently holding Della to her, her arms curved protectively around the tiny child. Sixteen years had gone by and she was back to relying on the kindness of others. She sighed.

He saw the pensive look on her face. She was probably having second thoughts. "Listen, I'm just going to make a call and get you some things."

"Things?" She looked at him, snapping out of her mood. "What things?"

"Well," he pointed to the baby, "Della needs something to sleep in. And I didn't see any clothes for her when you were packing."

She had wanted to buy clothes, but Alan always seemed to need the money for something else. Her own weakness at giving in to him plagued her. "I never got around to buying very much," she said defensively. But there had been no excuse, not for any of it.

There was no need for her to explain. His tone was

meant to reassure her. "Kathy'll have everything you need."

"Kathy?"

"Kathleen, my sister," he reminded her. "Never throws anything away. After three kids, her garage looks like a baby store." He started backing out the doorway. "Just hang on."

He disappeared from the room. "Just hang on," she echoed. She looked down at the baby. "Just what does he think we've been trying to do?"

The baby responded by trying to shove her fist into her mouth. Melissa stared at her, mystified. "You can't be hungry again. I just fed you."

Della began to whimper.

"Okay, okay." Melissa sat on the bed. It felt marvelously comfortable, not like the thin mattresses at the string of motels she had stayed in. She began unbuttoning her caftan. She had thought that the feeding had been over with rather quickly before. "I guess that was just the appetizer. You're ready for the main course now, aren't you?"

That was how he found her.

He hadn't meant to stare. He was bringing in the flower arrangement and coming to tell her that Kathy was going to be right over, propelled by curiosity because he purposely wouldn't explain anything to her. Del stopped two feet short of the doorway.

Melissa was sitting on the edge of the bed, half-turned from him, holding her child to her breast. The receiving blanket she had used earlier was in her lap.

Thinking she was alone, she hadn't draped it over her shoulder yet.

Del felt something tighten in his stomach. Longing, the likes of which he had never known, coursed through every part of his body at once. The pull was hot and demanding. And there was something more, something he couldn't quite identify yet. There was nothing he could do to protect himself against any of it.

Taking several steps back into the hall, Del cleared his throat before he approached the doorway.

Hearing him, Melissa quickly threw the blanket over her shoulder, covering herself and the suckling infant. She was watching as he entered.

Too bad everyday people weren't up for Academy Awards, he thought. His innocent act would certainly entitle him to at least a nomination. "Kathy's going to be right over."

"What did you tell her?"

She wouldn't know how to begin such a call. *Hello, I've just found this homeless woman and she needs everything.*

But Del made it sound all perfectly normal. "To bring over a portable crib, bottles, clothes and anything else she could think of that a three-day-old infant might need or want." He placed the flowers on top of the bureau. The pink-and-white carnations seemed to brighten the room. But not as much as she did.

"What did she say?" Although she could pretty well imagine.

He decided that Della could have the room next door. Melissa was going to need her sleep. She was beginning to look exhausted again. "That she'd be right over."

Just like that? What kind of people were these? No one she ever knew had been that outgoingly generous. "Didn't your request strike her as a little odd?"

He laughed, resting on the edge of the windowsill. "That's why she said she'd be right over. Kathy isn't the fastest person in the world. Unless she's being motivated by curiosity."

Melissa liked her immediately.

Kathleen Santini Cordell, a foot shorter than her brother, but just as dark in coloring, just as lively in temperament, swooped into Del's cluttered house, portable crib in tow, with three children following in her wake. Each was carrying something. The youngest, a girl of no more than two, was dragging a denim diaper bag filled with baby clothes. She was dropping a trail all through the living room as she came.

Melissa thought it rather blended in with the rest of the decor.

Kathleen set the folded crib against the side of the sofa. Del picked it up, ready to take it into the baby's room. Kathleen stopped him with the touch of her hand on his arm. "You've acquired a family since I last talked to you." Her words were for him, but the warm, encouraging smile was for Melissa. "Introduce me."

Del put down the crib. "Melissa Ryan, this is my bossy younger sister, Kathleen Cordell."

"Don't pay any attention to him." Kathleen waved at Del as he disappeared into the other room. "Nobody can get him to do anything he doesn't want to." Kathleen looked at the baby. "Can I hold him?"

"Her," Melissa corrected as she placed Della into Kathleen's ready arms.

"Even better." Kathleen held the baby up and took a deep whiff. "Oh, I love the smell of new babies." She rested Della against her shoulder. "That's the trap, you know. They smell so good, you want more. You forget that they grow up into whirling dervishes."

Holding Della, Kathleen looked at her trio who were fighting over which channel to watch on Del's large TV console. Yanking the remote control back and forth, the two boys knocked over a pyramid of magazines from the top of the television set. The periodicals tumbled to the floor, joining others that had gone before. The little girl was distracted by the magazines and started to go through them, while the boys continued to scuffle.

"Boys, stop that," Kathleen ordered. And they did. For three seconds. "Uh-oh."

Melissa looked at her, concerned. "What?"

Kathleen's hand was on Della's bottom. "She needs changing." She looked around at the mess in the living room. It was hard to tell what there was or wasn't available. "Got any diapers?"

Something else she had forgotten. "No."

"Lucky for you I stopped at the store on my way over," Kathleen said just as Del walked into the living room. "There's a box of disposable diapers in the car, Del." She turned toward her brother. "Go get it."

"See?" he said to Melissa as he stopped to kiss his sister's cheek. "Bossy." He left to retrieve the diapers. As always, Kathleen thought of everything.

Kathleen was trying not to be too obvious as she studied the woman on the sofa next to her. "How did you and Del meet?"

Kathleen looked so natural holding Della. Melissa wondered if she'd ever feel that at ease. "On the freeway."

"He gave you a ticket?"

"He delivered my baby."

Kathleen grinned broadly. "So you're the one."

"One what?" Melissa asked suspiciously. Just what had he been telling people about her?

"Del crowed about delivering a baby the other night to anyone who'd listen." She took another look at Della. "You do nice work," she commented to Melissa. "Are you visiting for a while?"

Visiting. That had a nice, nonjudgmental ring to it. "Yes, until I get back on my feet. Your brother was kind enough to offer me a place to stay. I was traveling in from Arizona when the baby decided she was going to be born ahead of schedule. I really don't know what I would have done without Del."

She stopped for breath, then realized just how much she had said. Why was she so inclined to talk

around Del and now his sister? Just what kind of per-
suasive powers did they have? She was usually so
closemouthed about everything. It was something in
their eyes, in their manner, she decided, that seemed
to coax the words out.

Kathleen smiled, not surprised. "That's Del, all
right."

"He's done this sort of thing before?" Maybe he
made a habit out of taking in women who were down
on their luck, she thought. The idea that she was just
like everyone else to him bothered her, even though
she knew it shouldn't.

The baby began to fuss over her wet diaper. Kathleen started to rock slightly as she gently patted the
little back. "Not exactly, but if anyone ever needed
a ride, or money to tide them over, or a place to crash,
Del was there for them. Drove Drew crazy."

"Drew?"

"One of my other brothers. He owned this house,
too." She remembered the arguments, though there
had never been any real friction. "Drew liked peace
and quiet. Del liked stepping into Saint Francis of
Assisi's sandals."

Were they talking about the same man? "He told
me he was wild."

Kathleen saw no contradiction. "So was Saint
Francis, in the beginning. The good streak was always
there, though." She rose from the sofa as she saw Del
return with the diapers. "Want my advice?" she
asked seriously.

Melissa was open to anything. "Please."

The solemn look left Kathleen's face and she grinned. "Run if squirrels and other fuzzy animals start appearing at the back door."

Del handed her the diaper bag by the plastic strap. "What are you telling her?"

"Just teaching her about Saint Francis of Assisi," Kathleen said innocently. She turned her attention to Della. "Let's go, young lady, we're going to get you changed." Kathleen began to leave the room, then turned toward Melissa. "What's her name?"

"Della."

"Uh-huh." There was a knowing smile on her lips as she walked out.

"I like your sister."

Del perched on the arm of the sofa, next to her. "Everyone does. She tends to take charge, but she's good at it."

Melissa looked up at him. "Runs in the family."

"You mean me?" He shook his head. "Naw, I'm the irresponsible one." He winked, and she could feel her stomach flutter again. Must be hunger, she hoped. "Just ask anyone."

"I already did." Her eyes indicated the direction his sister had taken.

"Sisters can't be trusted to tell the truth." There was a crash on the other side of the room. Jimmy and Stevie were fighting again, this time over one of Del's prized toy trains that stood on display. Stevie landed, bottom first, on the remote control. Del winced. "Hey, you little monsters, the trip to the amusement park at the end of the month is off if either of you jam my controls.''

She sincerely doubted, as she watched him cross the room to intervene, that anything could ever jam his controls.

Chapter Six

There was something about the night that always seemed to undermine her confidence and magnify any fears that might be lurking in the hidden chambers of her mind. Knowing that her feelings traced their roots back to her childhood, when she had fearfully stood guard by the window, waiting and watching for her mother to return from one of her nightlong binges, didn't ameliorate the feelings of loneliness, of helplessness she was now experiencing. If she was going to waver in her convictions, it almost always happened after dusk.

Such as now.

She drew the drapes shut in her bedroom, then stood, fidgeting with the cord. What did she really know about this man whose house she had entered so freely?

All right, so he was a policeman. And yes, he had

a nice smile. A nice smile, a nice sister and a nice house. But that didn't mean he couldn't turn on her suddenly. Somebody somewhere along the line must have thought the Boston Strangler was nice, too. And trustworthy.

When she had agreed to this arrangement yesterday it was because she had been desperate. She had nowhere to turn. He was her one option, and she had firmly believed that she could handle herself in any situation if he decided to try anything.

She looked around the bedroom nervously, her tension in sharp contrast to the cheery decor. Antsy, she plucked at the flowers on the bureau.

He *was* a policeman, trained in all sorts of body holds. And she was trained to teach children. That didn't exactly give them an equal footing as far as the matter of physical defense if he tried to seduce her.

Melissa caught a glimpse of herself in the mirror. She moved aside the vase and looked at her reflection more closely. Her hair looked more like a wild mane, and there were dark smudges beneath her eyes, the ones that always appeared when she was exhausted.

Tried to seduce her? The man should probably be heading for the hills. *Give yourself a lot of credit, don't you? You look like something the cat dragged in on a bad day.* There was no doubt in her mind that Del could do better than this without really trying, if he was looking for female companionship.

She ran her hand over her arms, not from any chill

without, but from the one she felt within. She was restless and tired at the same time.

And embarrassed again, embarrassed because she needed help. Except for those times she was foisted on Aunt Julia and Uncle Henry, forced to accept their charity, she had all but raised herself. She was proud of that. This was a humiliating situation for her to be in. Damn Alan, damn his cold heart for taking everything.

Most of all, damn her for believing.

She jumped and accidentally hit the vase with her elbow when she heard the light knock on her door. It tottered precariously. She steadied it with shaking hands.

Calm down. If he was going to try anything, he wouldn't have knocked first.

She cleared her throat and tried to sound confident. "Come in."

The door eased open as she held her breath. She let it go slowly when she saw him carrying a tray. It was set for dinner for one.

He saw her eyeing the tray. "I thought you might be hungry."

The aroma had her drawing closer. "That smells like—Stroganoff?"

She raised her eyes to his face quizzically. It wasn't the type of thing she expected a bachelor to just whip up. Ham and cheese on rye was more in keeping with the surroundings she found here. If Alan was feeling especially creative, he added mustard and lettuce. But a hot meal? Never.

"It is." Del set the tray on the bed. He had expected to find her in it and was surprised that she was pacing around the room. "I had some left over from the other day, but it tastes better with time—up to a point." He grinned. "It hasn't reached that point yet. Try some," he urged.

Sitting on the edge of the bed, she took a small taste. She'd had no idea that she even had an appetite until she took the first bite. It begged for a second and a third to follow in its wake. She'd been so wound up in her problem, she'd forgotten to be hungry. She was ravenous.

He was watching her eat. There was obvious pleasure on his face. It made her feel self-conscious. She took a sip of the tea he'd brought in to quench the sudden dryness in her mouth. The dryness that seemed to come every time he looked at her. "This is very good. Did your sister make it?"

"Kathleen?" He started to laugh, vividly remembering Kathleen's last efforts at something that didn't have to be defrosted or taken out of a can. Dennis had wound up in the emergency room, treated for acute gastric distress. "Much to Ma's dismay, Kathleen was the only one of us who didn't learn how to cook." He watched her take another forkful and thought that he could watch her eat all evening. He leaned back on the bed. "I made it."

Melissa's eyes narrowed. "You?" She'd expected him to say he brought home dinners from his mother's. At the last school where she'd worked, one of the aides had a mother who cooked for him every week and stocked his freezer from weekend to weekend.

Del sat up, amused at her startled reaction. "You say that like it's impossible."

"No, not impossible. I just thought that a man who couldn't keep house—" The words slipped out without her wanting them to. She hadn't meant that to sound the way it did. He was feeding her and she was insulting him. "I mean—"

But he took no offense. "You mean that you thought a man who's a slob can't cook."

She flushed, and he found the color bewitching on her. "Not in those words, but, well…yes."

He laughed. "The two are mutually exclusive."

"Apparently." Melissa looked down at the plate on the tray and realized that she had finished it all. And longed for more. "I guess I should have waited until I got to the table."

He took the tray and placed it on the side of the bed for the time being. "If I had wanted you at the table, I wouldn't have served you here."

Their eyes locked for a moment and she couldn't make herself look away, even though she knew she should. His eyes were so bright and blue they were almost magnetic. "Where is it that you want me?"

"In bed." That sounded exactly the way he meant it, but only to himself, he hoped. He didn't want Melissa thinking that he had her here for any ulterior motives. "For your own good."

So, there it was. Melissa took a deep breath, knowing she had to brazen this out. "I've never heard it put that way before.'' She sat up, her back straight as a rod. Indignation flashed in her eyes.

"I meant as in sleep," he corrected.

She frowned, her anger dying. She couldn't be angry if he hadn't meant what she thought he had meant. "I don't understand."

"Apparently." He placed his hands on her arm and found it rigid with tension. "I'm trying to tell you that I want you to get your rest."

He really was too good to be true. She felt foolish. "And nothing more?"

Oh, there's more, lots more, but not now. "If there is to be more, Melissa, it'll come when you're free. And ready."

Her ruse had worked. He thought she was married. Why did that make her feel so guilty? "By free, you mean divorced?"

He nodded. "Legally separated, wanting to be separated, something." He wanted her to understand, to feel at ease. "I don't poach on another man's territory," he told her softly.

"You make me sound like a deer."

He couldn't help himself. Slowly he ran the back of his hand along her cheek, needing to feel her skin, needing just the slightest bit of male-female contact, even though he had promised himself that he would maintain distance. "Dear, not deer. With an *ea*."

Her guilt grew. She didn't understand someone like Del. Not anymore. She was afraid to believe that he was what he appeared to be. For if she did, her defenses would wane and she would be helpless. She frowned. "Don't be nice to me, Santini."

How could he help being nice to her? He only wished that the wariness would leave her eyes. He wanted her to trust him, and chafed at his own impatience. "Want me to get out the whip and the chains?"

"You're laughing at me."

"No, I'm trying to get you to laugh, period. It's a beautiful sound, and I'd really like to hear it again." Del rose, and the tray came crashing down at his feet. He had forgotten all about it. The surprise on his face made Melissa laugh. "Not particularly at my expense, though," he added as he bent to pick up the fallen things.

"No, let me. It's my fault." She was on her knees beside him, her hands getting in his way. Her body getting in his way. As they both reached for the plate together, he grinned, tugging it in his direction. "Best two out of three."

Her hand was still on the plate. "Best two out of three what?"

He couldn't help himself. Her mouth was too close, the room was too small. And his needs and desires were too great. Everything conspired against his good intentions. Before he knew it, the plate had fallen back to the floor, hitting the tray with a clatter, and his hands were on her arms, as if to push her away. As if to push away temptation.

But he didn't.

Rather than pushing, he was holding her in place,

steadying her, steadying himself. His heart pounding in his ears, his mouth covered hers as if his very life would fade from this earth if he didn't kiss her this instant.

It was everything he had thought it would be. And more. So much more. He tried to absorb it all, the feel, the taste. The thrill. It was as if he'd never kissed a woman before, never understood what could happen to him if he did. He didn't fully understand now. He only knew that he was lost and in her power.

His hands dived into her hair as he cupped the back of her head, tilting her so that he could deepen the kiss and try vainly to get his fill.

He knew it would never happen.

The tightrope she had been precariously balancing herself on snapped. Melissa was falling headlong into an abyss, frightened and exhilarated and completely confused. She had to stop him.

She couldn't stop him.

She wouldn't let him stop. Her arms were suddenly traveling up his back as she clung to him, clung to the strength she found in his kiss. The edgy taste of passion excited her even as she knew she should break free.

He brought her up to her knees, still holding her, the tray between them on the floor. The world between them.

Nothing but raw need between them.

He had never had such little control over himself before. It was frightening, like free-falling without knowing if his chute was going to open. He had no idea if he was even wearing one.

Del pulled away from her before he did something he felt Melissa was not going to forgive him for. He wanted to make love with her here, now, but there was a host of reasons why he couldn't. Physically she wasn't ready—wouldn't be for several weeks. But more important than that, she wasn't ready emotionally. He had to remember that, remember that she was married and not his to have. Yet.

But a man could only hold back so much, and right now he knew he was tottering dangerously at the breaking point.

"I'm sorry." Del dragged a hand through his hair, his breath ragged. He looked at her, at the way her eyes were still slightly dazed, slightly unfocused. At her lips, which were redder, blurred from the pressure of his. "No, I'm not. I'm not sorry I kissed you. I'm only sorry that the circumstances aren't right and that you're married."

The lie burned. She was torn between the truth and self-preservation. "I—"

"Yes?"

Della was beginning to cry in the other room. Melissa retreated. It was better this way. "I had better tend to the baby."

Control was not as easily regained as he would've liked, but he managed. "Right." He rocked back on his heels, picking up the silverware and dropping the utensils on the tray.

Guilt raced through her, forging a fiery path. Guilt

for letting him believe a lie. Guilt for letting him kiss her.

Guilt for liking it.

She was tired of having feelings, tired of emotions that swept through her like a riptide, sucking out everything she had to give.

Del rose with the tray in his hands. "See you in the morning."

"Good night." Her voice followed him out. By the time he left the room, he'd managed to steady his breathing. His pulse was another matter entirely.

Melissa quickly went into the other room to check on the baby, grateful that she had someone else to occupy her mind.

But Della's cries had stopped and she had fallen asleep again. Melissa stood watching her, trying to gain peace. She ran her hand along the smooth white railing, fighting back emotions that begged to be set free. The sight of her baby soothed her for a moment, but nothing was going to soothe the ache that had suddenly sprung up within her. The ache that Del's kiss had aroused.

What was the matter with her? When would she learn? Here she was, ready to buy into another pipe dream, another fantasy of her own making. How many times did she have to get bashed over the head before she stopped believing in happy endings? Stopped believing that there was something at the end of the rainbow besides dirt and grass?

Oh, but when Del had kissed her, the world had tilted, things had stirred within her.

Hope had tried to break loose.

And damn, hot tears stung her eyes as she clenched her hands. She knew there wasn't any hope left. Not anywhere. She wasn't going to be hurt again. She wasn't. Never again. All she had to do was stop her own vulnerability, her own needs, from eating through the coat of armor she kept trying to construct around her heart.

Del was being kind right now. But he was a man and by definition out for himself. Sooner or later, when she was least prepared, it would come through. He'd hurt her.

"They're all out for themselves, Missy, just you remember that."

Her mother's voice echoed in the recesses of her mind, haunting her. She hadn't believed then, had refused to believe, despite everything that had happened to her mother. Despite the way her mother had gone on being used by the men who came in and out of her life as she sought someone to love her.

That was her mother, Melissa had told herself. It would be different for her.

And then she had met Alan. Alan who lit up her skies and made her believe that things were going to be wonderful from now on. When he left so abruptly, the lesson finally came home.

If there was a good man out there somewhere, she thought, unconsciously looking over her shoulder toward Del's room, then why hadn't he come while she could still believe that happiness was possible?

The emptiness within her made her ache, tearing

away at her heart, threatening to engulf it in its own blackness. She'd feel better after a night's sleep, she told herself. She always did. Turning, she began to silently creep from the room.

When she reached the door, Della started to cry.

Melissa crossed back to the crib. "So you have radar, do you?" she murmured, picking up the tiny bundle. "Shh, I'm here. I'm here." She began to walk the floor. "I'll always be here for you. Don't you worry."

Del was in the kitchen, stacking the plates in the sink when he heard the baby cry. His first instinct was to go to Della, but he stopped himself. Melissa was there. And right now, he was certain she needed her space.

He upbraided himself again for his lack of self-control, for his insensitivity. How could he have taken advantage of her while she was so defenseless? Wanting her wasn't an excuse. She was going to be twice as leery of him from now on. Instead of gaining her trust, he'd messed things up and done just the opposite. He was going to have to tread twice as gently to make up for whatever there was in her life that had gotten her to this crossroads, alone and wary of everyone and everything.

With a sigh, he dropped the tray on the table. It landed on top of the sports section from last Sunday's newspaper.

Yet the woman he'd kissed just a few minutes ago had been full of passion, of needs, and he could fill them so easily. Without even trying.

But he'd have to try. Try harder. He could always size things up quickly, efficiently, and he knew now that there was to be "something" between them. Whether it was a relationship or more depended, he felt, entirely on what happened here and now in the next few weeks.

Del looked at the sink. The dishes were beginning to form a pyramid. He really should get to them. Tomorrow. Tomorrow was always good.

He heard the baby let out with a loud wail and started, then laughed at himself. All this was still new to him. For a minute, he had forgotten about the baby.

Della.

How strange to have another human being running around, named after him. Well, not running, he amended. That wouldn't happen for at least a year. Of course, he was Jimmy's godfather, but it wasn't quite the same thing as having someone named after him. That was special.

Del stopped outside the baby's door. It was cracked open, only partially shut. He forced himself to knock rather than just walk in. The room had been Drew's before he moved out last year, and Del was used to just barging in. His family had that kind of relationship, barging into one another's lives whenever and wherever the need arose. That was where the loving part came in.

When he knocked, there was no answer. He wondered if she'd heard him. He knocked again. "Melissa, do you need anything?" He reached for the doorknob, turning it, ready to come in.

"No!" She almost shouted. She lowered her voice. "Nothing."

The answer had come a little too fast, a little too emphatically. She was reacting to the kiss, he thought ruefully, releasing the doorknob. *Nice going, Santini. Next you'll be scaring off little children.*

He bit his lip and tried again. "Do you want me to walk her?"

She turned, watching the door, wanting him to come in. Wanting him to go away. "What?"

"While you get some rest," he explained. He leaned his head against the wall next to the door. "Melissa, could I come in?"

She knew that one word would be all it took to bring him. She shut her eyes, holding Della to her breast like a shield. "I'd really rather you didn't right now."

He understood and had only himself to blame. "Right." Fisted hands shoved into his pockets. "See you in the morning."

She opened her eyes. Through the space left between the door and the doorjamb, she saw his shadow on the floor. She turned and walked in the other direction, wishing again that he'd go away. Wishing that the things that were churning inside of her would go away as well.

She might, she thought with a touch of bitterness, just as well have wished to have been the Queen of England. She probably would have stood a better chance of getting her wish granted then.

"Hush, hush," she murmured to her daughter,

holding her close as she walked in a circle around the crib. "It'll be all right. I promise. Everything's going to be all right. I won't let you down."

Melissa was making the promise to herself as much as she was to her daughter, Del thought as he stood in the hallway and listened. And he promised himself that her words were true.

"Neither will I, Melissa," he said very softly to the woman on the other side of the door, knowing she couldn't hear him. "And neither will I."

Leaving the light on in the hall, instinctively knowing it somehow made her feel better, Del turned and walked very quietly to his room. But he had a feeling that he was going to get very little sleep tonight, even if the baby did stop crying.

Chapter Seven

Time seemed to inch by, each minute multiplying itself a hundredfold, before Della finally fell asleep and remained asleep. Melissa literally tiptoed out of the room. Tired beyond her wildest imagination, she hardly had enough energy to strip her clothes off and put on her nightgown.

As she crawled into her bed, sliding beneath the cool navy sheets, Melissa silently blessed the fact that Del had been intuitive enough to give her a separate bedroom. If Della was in the same room with her, Melissa knew she'd be listening to the baby's every sound, tense, waiting for her to wake up again. The silence within her own room was blissfully comforting. Settling back, she calculated that she had approximately four hours or so before Della's next performance.

She was asleep in two minutes.

Della's cries woke Melissa from a deep, almost drugged sleep. She turned toward the nightstand to look at the clock. It wasn't there.

Where was she?

Slowly, through the fog of sleep, her thoughts straggled in, clumsily fitting together. She was in Del's house. The realization had her mind snapping to attention. Moonlight streamed in through the partially separated curtains. She reached for her wristwatch on the nightstand, trying to focus on the numbers. Twelve o'clock. Oh God, she'd only been asleep for fifteen minutes. She looked again in disbelief. No, it was two o'clock, not twelve. That meant she'd had a little more than two hours' sleep. She supposed that was something.

Melissa sat up in bed, trying to get oriented. She dragged her hand through her hair, pushing the dark mane away from her face. The baby wasn't due for another feeding for at least two hours.

"I suppose you can't tell time yet, huh?" she murmured to her absent daughter. Eyes still unfocused, Melissa looked at the wall that separated the two rooms.

She suddenly remembered Del. The baby was going to wake him up, if she hadn't already. That would be a terrible way to repay him after he had put himself out like this.

Grabbing her robe from the edge of her bed, Melissa had only shoved one arm into a sleeve before she reached the baby's room. The light robe floated behind her like a bright yellow streamer.

Della's door was open. And she had company.

Melissa blinked, wondering if she was still asleep and dreaming. It was the kind of thing she would have fantasized about. Del was in the room, bare-chested and wearing what looked like a very worn-out pair of jeans. Maybe he used them as pajamas, she thought, her heart stirring at the sight of the man with the tiny baby in his arms. He was pacing slowly.

And singing. Melissa's mouth curved.

It was a soft lullaby, a little off-key, but it sounded beautiful to Melissa. Tears suddenly rose to her eyes.

Damn unpredictable hormones, she thought, always messing her up at the wrong time. She shouldn't be crying because some man was singing to her child.

But she was.

Because it made her remember all the things she had thought would be hers one day. And all the things that weren't. All her life she had wanted a scene like this, dreamed of one like this. Her husband singing to her baby. Instead it was an off-duty policeman she hadn't known a week ago. A man just passing through her life out of the goodness of his heart. A man who would be the best father any little girl could ask for.

She sniffed and rubbed the heel of her hand hard across her face, wiping the tears away.

Turning, Del saw Melissa standing in the doorway, her robe hanging half off her body, trailing down her arm. The light was still on in the hallway, just as he'd left it. It filtered through her nightgown, outlining her body in gentle, mouth-watering hues.

Del's mouth turned to dust as sensations rippled

through him, hardening his body, making him ache. Without thinking, he automatically held Della tighter to keep from dropping her. Uncomfortable, the baby whimpered.

"Sorry," he murmured to Della under his breath, loosening his hold. It was himself he needed to get a tighter hold on, not the baby.

He cleared his throat, then swallowed, afraid his voice would crack if he attempted to say more than a couple of words. Even so soon after childbirth, Melissa had the body of a goddess, meant for worship. Desire began to eat away at every fiber of his being.

He couldn't recall when he had ever been this aroused, this needy. Always before, desire had been something very pleasant, but something he could easily push aside if the occasion wasn't right. He could no more push this aside than if it was a giant boulder, blocking his every path of escape. Remembering to keep his distance was getting harder and harder for him.

Feeling ignored, Della let out with a wail that was lusty for one her size.

Del found his tongue and untied it. "Umm, I guess she doesn't care for off-key lullabies."

Even in the dark, with the faintest hint of moonlight coming in from the window, Melissa had seen the way he looked at her. It wasn't good, not for her. It drew her in when she had no business being drawn. Yet she couldn't deny that it made her glad as well. It made her feel like a woman. His look was warm, penetrating. It was as if he was touching something inside her that was struggling so hard to stay alive.

She took a step forward and the robe brushed against the back of her legs. She flushed, realizing that she was still only half wearing it. Putting it on, she secured the robe at her waist. Then crossing to Del, she took her daughter from his arms.

"Here, you shouldn't have to do this. You've been too kind already."

He hadn't realized how heavy seven pounds two ounces could grow to be after half an hour. Still, he was loath to give Della up. "There's no such thing as being too kind. Too pushy maybe, but not too kind."

Not to you, he added silently, but knew she wasn't ready to hear that.

Oh, please, she thought. *Please don't be nice to me like this. I've got no defenses left and I need them, against you, against me. I can't let things happen again, not until I can get myself together.*

Del saw the flash of fear in her eyes. Lightly, because he couldn't resist, he touched her arm. Even that was too much temptation. He took a step back, not trusting himself so close to her.

Melissa flashed a grateful smile and he knew it was going to be all right. For now.

He nodded toward the baby. "I changed her, but I think she might be hungry. Or maybe crying was her defense against my singing."

She tried to picture him changing Della's diaper,

and a grin lifted the corners of her mouth. "Where did you learn that? The lullaby," she clarified.

The song had come to him without effort, without thought. It was forever nestled away in the corners of his mind.

"Standing over four cribs. That's the song my mother always sang. Over and over again. Never tried another. I guess she figured we'd fall asleep out of boredom." He knew he should go. He'd hardly had any sleep and he'd be dead on his feet at work. But he wanted to stay. "Sure you don't need anything?"

"No." This time, she said the word softly, with thanks. "You keep asking me that."

"It's the public servant in me," he said with a wink. "And you keep saying no," he pointed out. Leaning against the doorjamb, he folded his arms across his chest. "You don't like asking for help."

The clothes he'd worn before hadn't given her a clear picture of the man beneath. The low-slung jeans fit snugly, like a second skin, accenting slender hips and well-formed legs. His lightly haired chest was defined with ridges and muscles that made her fingers long to touch. She began to walk. Because the baby needed soothing. And in deference to survival. "Does anyone?"

"You'd be surprised."

She tried to concentrate on his words, on the situation, anything other than the fact that he was so handsome and so very close. "Well, I don't. Asking means you're weak."

"Asking means you're human. Everyone needs a

little help sometime." Not being able to resist, warning himself to go slowly, he came to her. "I'll see you in the morning." So saying, he brushed the lightest of kisses against her lips.

Just the slightest of encounters.

It was enough to send the alarms ringing through his body. He smiled softly into her upturned face. "See if you can get some rest. Me—" he was already backing away "—I'm going to take a cold shower."

Maybe two cold showers, he thought as he kept walking.

Her lips still carried the imprint of his first kiss. This kiss, faster than the one before, almost chaste in comparison, told her that she was in trouble. Not from him. From herself. She wanted too much, yearned too much, and therefore was much too vulnerable.

Maybe, she thought as she sat down with Della, preparing to nurse her, these were just misplaced emotions and what she was really feeling was only gratitude.

As long as she believed that, held on to that, she'd be all right. She turned her attention to Della and forced herself to think of no one and nothing else.

Del wondered if she'd still be there. He tried not to pay attention to the fear that surrounded that question as he drove away from the precinct.

Though she was trying so hard to put up a strong front, he'd seen more than once the fear that was in her eyes. She reminded him of a doe, ready to flee at the slightest provocation.

And he certainly had been provoking last night, he thought. Nothing light-handed about him.

Before going home, he stopped at his uncle's restaurant to pick up a pizza. He had told Melissa this morning on his way out that he'd take care of dinner, ordering her not to cook anything. The aroma of cheese and pepperoni filled his small car now. Normally it was enough to make him hungry, but he was too preoccupied.

Would he be eating it alone? He took a turn and sped up. Melissa had nowhere to go, but that hadn't stopped people on the run before. And she was on the run. From something.

From someone.

Who? Her husband? Herself? He knew nothing about her, yet he felt he knew everything that mattered. She was hurt, she was alone and she needed someone. That was enough for him.

When he pulled into his driveway the relief that washed over him was overwhelming. The beaten-looking silver van was still there, sagging in places like a tired animal who had given more than what was required of it. He'd probably get a note from the Homeowners' Association in his mailbox about it, he thought, getting out of the car. In his estimation the Homeowner's Association was a group of conservative-minded people whose sole calling in life was to keep the houses within The Naranjos development looking neat, tidy and almost identical.

If he thought about it at length, the strict regulations bothered his sense of independence. But the mortgage payments were more than reasonable, so he let things slide.

You make compromises, he thought, to get on in life. He hoped that Melissa realized that. Balancing the hot pizza in one hand, he opened the door.

And then stopped dead.

"I don't think we're in Kansas anymore, Toto" he muttered under his breath as he looked around, dazed. "Must be the right house," he reassured himself. "The key fits."

Because heat was beginning to penetrate from the box to his fingers, he set the pizza on the coffee table. A coffee table now denuded of newspapers, magazines and discarded clothing. There wasn't a thing on the coffee table except for a shine.

Hands on his hips, Del slowly scanned the living room. He tried to put a fix on a time when he'd last seen it looking like this. The answer was easy. Never. Neither he nor Drew was much at housekeeping, and things just had a tendency to pile up, despite their halfhearted efforts at cleaning.

The room was immaculate.

It was also quiet. Too quiet.

He didn't hear the baby crying. He didn't hear anyone. His adrenaline began to hum. It wasn't as if he had sneaked in through the window. She must have heard him come in.

If she was home.

Looking over his shoulder, he glanced out the large bay window facing the front. Her van was still where he'd seen it in the driveway, but that didn't really mean anything. Maybe it wasn't working. He had had trouble getting it started when he had driven it here from the hospital. Maybe she had just called a cab.

With what? She didn't have any money to pay a cab driver.

He remembered the money he had stashed in the back of a drawer in his room, emergency money in case he or someone he knew needed a quick loan. His jaw tightened. He refused to believe she'd take it.

"Melissa!"

Where *was* she? Hurrying, he checked Della's room first. Then let out a sigh. The baby was sleeping peacefully in her crib, her bottom raised as she huddled in a comfortable spot on her tummy.

She wouldn't have left the baby, would she? He thought of the way Melissa had held the infant to her breast. No, she'd never do that. So where was she?

Easing the door closed behind him, Del lowered his voice as he called again. "Melissa?"

A muffled answer came in reply, from the direction of the kitchen.

The kitchen was located in the back end of the house, looking out on a small but sunny garden. Following the sound of what he hoped was her voice, Del walked into the kitchen. That was when he saw her.

Or the back part of her. It wasn't a bad view to encounter. Her seat trim, well rounded. She fit her jeans rather nicely, especially considering the fact that she had just had Della. All that extra weight she had been carrying must have just been the baby.

The rest of Melissa was hidden. She was kneeling on the floor, her head deep in the recesses of the refrigerator. A pink pan of what had once been soapy water but now resembled sludge was next to her, a sponge helplessly bobbing up and down in the murky sea. He recognized the pan from the hospital, part of the things they had taken with them in the care package. It hadn't been meant to be used for washing out the interior of a refrigerator.

Relieved, intrigued, Del squatted down next to her. "What are you doing?"

Her hair was pulled back from her face, carelessly bound with a colored rubber band she'd found in a kitchen drawer. She turned and looked over her shoulder. "Gathering penicillin."

With a sigh, she sat back and wiped the perspiration from her forehead. She'd been cleaning for most of the day, in between taking care of Della. Della hadn't required very much of her. The baby's game plan seemed to be sleeping through most of the day and staying up at night. Della had all the signs of being a nocturnal creature. She'd given birth to a seven pound two ounce cuddly hamster.

Melissa paused as she narrowed her eyes and looked at Del. How could one man be responsible for so much of a mess? She pulled what might have been the remains of a celery stalk from the bottom crisper. Nothing in it had been. "How long has it been since you cleaned this refrigerator out, Santini?"

He shrugged, then smiled as he tucked a loose

strand of hair behind her ear. "We bought it when we bought the house."

She stared at him, her eyes large. "And you haven't cleaned it since then?"

He took the stalk from her and tossed it in the direction of the garbage pail. It missed. "Never got around to it. What do you think you're doing?"

"Making your house safe for humanity." She eyed the fallen stalk. She'd spent half an hour scrubbing grease marks off the kitchen floor. She didn't appreciate having celery on it now.

He looked to see what she was staring at. Obligingly he got up, picked the stalk off the floor and tossed it into the pail, then turned his attention back to her. "I thought I told you to rest."

She looked at the refrigerator. It was as clean as it was going to get. She rose to her feet, stretching. "I can't do that in a mess. No offense."

"No offense." He turned before the sight of her breasts straining against the thin cotton shirt made him lose his train of thought and his control. "You didn't have to clean the whole house."

Melissa shrugged, carrying the pink pail to the bathroom. She poured the contents down the toilet, hanging on to the sponge. "I can't seem to stop myself once I get started."

He followed her. "I'll remember that." His eyes danced with humor as she turned to give him a quizzical look. "Come with me." He took the pail out of her hands, then laced his fingers with hers.

His hand felt good in hers. Too good. "Where're we going?"

"To retire your sponge." He tossed the pail on the kitchen counter and pulled out a chair for her. "I brought pizza for dinner."

She smiled as she dropped into the chair. "Sounds heavenly."

Absently he wondered where everything was. The kitchen was as neat as every other room now. He imagined that it would all turn up eventually. Maybe when he opened a closet, everything would come tumbling down on him, like a cartoon scene. She had to have put his things somewhere. Right now, he just wanted to get on with dinner. And to talk to her.

He crossed back to the living room and retrieved the pizza from the coffee table, bringing it to the kitchen. Her last ounce of oomph apparently having suddenly evaporated, she was sitting exactly where he had left her.

Del placed the pizza in front of her, then opened the box. Her eyes glowed when she saw the huge pie, smothered with cheese and pepperoni.

"You know, you really should be resting." He lifted the pizza out of the box, then slid the carton to the far side of the table. "The mess wasn't going anywhere."

"I wouldn't have taken bets on that. Some of it looked as if it had legs." Then her smile faded a little as she looked at him, her eyes serious. "I don't have any money yet—"

"I didn't exactly expect you to earn any while I was on duty."

She pushed on doggedly. "—and I wanted to start paying you back. I told you, I don't like owing." She rose, about to get two plates and some silverware. "And this was the only way I have." She gestured around the room.

She was moving again. Any minute, another rag would be in her hand and she'd be pushing around imaginary dust. Placing a hand on each shoulder, he forcibly pushed her back into her chair. "Sit."

He turned to get a couple of dishes from the dish rack and found that it was empty. She had not only washed all the dishes, she had put them away as well.

Mystified, he went to the cabinet and found everything was stacked there. His cabinet hadn't been full of clean dishes since—

He tried to think and realized that it never had been full of dishes. He and his brother had moved in, acquiring things as they went along. But the dishes had never completely found their way into the cabinet. To the rack in the sink was the best they had managed.

He took out two plates and placed them on the table. "You don't have to pay me back," he told her, though he was beginning to think saying it did no good. Gingerly, since it was still hot, he pulled the first piece free of the pie and placed it on her plate. "I'm not about to charge interest. And I won't foreclose on the old mansion, Little Nell."

She took a bite and found that she was having trouble getting to the end of the strand of cheese. She broke it with her fingertips and swallowed. "What's that supposed to mean?"

Taking a piece for himself, Del straddled the chair next to hers. "Didn't you ever watch Mighty Mouse cartoons as a kid?"

She shook her head. "No."

He was more interested in her than the pizza. "What did you do as a kid?"

The second bite was just as troublesome, just as delicious as the first. "Grow up."

Things were beginning to fall into place and make sense. "I think you need a trip to Disneyland along with my nephews and niece. I'm taking them at the end of the month. Della should be ready for her first experience at the Magic Kingdom by then."

He certainly wasn't very realistic for a policeman, was he? But she realized that it was one of the things she found most attractive about him. "She'll only be three weeks old."

"Old enough." He watched her eat with obvious relish. She had sauce on the corner of her mouth. He licked the tip of his pinky, then slowly brushed it along the curve of her lips, his eyes on hers.

As she watched, her heart lodged in her throat, he placed the finger in his mouth. She thought she'd stopped breathing by then.

"Isn't it terrific?" he asked.

She didn't know if he meant the pizza, or being here with him. She said yes to both. "You make this, too?" she stammered as an afterthought, remembering last night's meal.

He tore his eyes away from her face, afraid he was ready to sample something far more delectable than pizza. "Nope, my Uncle Fazio did. He makes pizza the way they do in New York. One continuous piece of cheese from beginning to end." He grinned, taking a bite to prove his point.

He had just gotten up to get a couple of cans of soda from the freshly cleaned refrigerator when the doorbell rang. He wasn't expecting anyone. He grumbled under his breath, placing the cans on the table.

"If it's some college kid selling subscriptions door-to-door to get points for a free cruise to Hawaii, he's going to be very disappointed," he told Melissa, heading toward the doorway. "I'll be right back."

Striding across the hallway, he reached the front door and threw it open, ready to evict anyone who stood on his doorstep.

The eviction notice disintegrated as he looked at the small, vivacious-looking woman on his doorstep.

"Oh. Hi, Ma."

Chapter Eight

Her waist was still trim, her skin still firm and glowing. She looked more like his older sister than his mother. At fifty-three, Gina Delveccio Santini appeared only a shade older than when Guiseppe Santini first saw her behind the counter of her father's restaurant thirty-two years ago. And she was still every bit as sharp, every bit as vibrant.

Gina leveled a piercing look at her son, the look that had gotten him to confess putting a laxative into Father Lehey's coffee cake when he was fourteen. The look that demanded nothing short of the truth from him. And quickly, if he knew what was good for him.

"Don't give me that innocent 'Hi, Ma' business." She placed her hands on her hips, her small purse swinging from her wrist. "Kathleen tells me that you called her for diapers, baby bottles and cribs." Kathleen had told her a lot more than that, but Gina had come to see for herself what Del was up to.

"Crib," he corrected. He'd wondered what had taken his mother so long to get here. Kathleen wasn't one to keep news to herself, and she had known about Melissa for twenty-four hours. Del was surprised his mother hadn't turned up on his doorstep at dawn. "Only one, Ma."

"Good." She moved him aside with the back of her hand as she marched in. Gina looked around in amazement. There wasn't anything lying around. No clutter, no mess. For once she didn't have to carefully pick her way through the room. "Then I know you're not starting a foundling home." She turned and faced him squarely. "What is going on, Del? The house is clean."

"Can't put anything over on you, can I, Ma?" He kissed her cheek fondly. "Want to come in for some pizza?" He gestured toward the kitchen.

"I want to come in for some answers." Gina paused, then relented. She cocked her head. "Uncle Fazio's?"

Del spread his hands wide. "Would I go anywhere else?"

Gina inclined her head, her short, stylishly cut black hair bobbing about her ears. There were only a few gray hairs sprinkled here and there, and they complemented rather than detracted from her looks. How she avoided being completely gray with a son like him, she had said to Del countless times, she had no idea. "Well, maybe just a slice."

When they walked into the kitchen, Melissa's place was empty. Del wondered if she had heard his mother and left the room suddenly, or if she had just found something else to clean.

Gina eyed the place setting suspiciously. "You were expecting me?"

"No, Ma." He knew his mother enjoyed playing the part of the inquisitor. She called it detective work, but it was a great deal more than that. He wasn't about to explain anything to her unless she asked him outright.

"But another place is set."

"Yes."

Gina picked up a napkin and looked at it closely. "The baby isn't using lipstick yet, is she?"

"No, Ma."

Gina let the napkin drop back to the table and threw up her hands. "Are we going to go on with questions and answers or are you going to tell me something that involves more than one word at a time?"

Where *was* Melissa? he wondered as he sat across from his mother. He could see that Gina was bursting with curiosity, but wouldn't admit it. He was enjoying this exchange between them more than just a little. "I've been giving you two-word answers."

Gina's eyes narrowed as she took a slice of pizza and broke off a piece of the crust. Slowly she raised it to her mouth, all the while waiting for her son to speak. She didn't want her mouth full of food if he said anything. She wanted to be ready to answer.

"You've been giving me nothing but heartache

since the day you were born, all ten and a half pounds of you." She wiped her fingers on the napkin. "So, where is this baby and her mother?" she asked impatiently. If she was a grandmother again, she wanted to know. Now. She eyed Del expectantly.

Del shrugged, playing the scene out. He loved his mother dearly, but she would have been disappointed if she didn't have to drag things out of him. It would spoil it for her.

"In the other room, I would imagine." Maybe Della had cried while he was answering the door. That would explain Melissa's absence. But if the baby was crying, why didn't he hear her?

Gina shook her head. "You'll never make a detective with police work that shoddy. That wasn't the way your father did things, God rest his soul." She leaned forward across the table, her eyes pinning her son. "He also didn't have babies all over the house before he got married."

He thought of the way Melissa had looked in the hospital room, alone, lost. There was no way he would have left her. "This was unavoidable, Ma."

Gina rolled her eyes and glanced toward the ceiling. "You hear, Guiseppe? Unavoidable." She sighed dramatically. "Just like your Uncle Joey." The memory of her younger brother made her shake her head. "Always thought with another part of his anatomy. What your grandmother didn't go through."

It was time to put her out of her misery. Or call the curtain down on her performance as the wronged mother. "It's not my baby."

"It's not?" Del definitely heard a hopeful note in her voice.

"No," Melissa said as she walked into the kitchen with Della in her arms. "It's not." Was this another relative? she wondered. They kept popping up. She couldn't help but envy him. "He just delivered it."

Gina was still unconvinced. She had six children and they had all tried their hand at putting something over on her at one time or another. And none so often or so successfully as Del. She looked at him now, wanting the truth. "Like the stork?"

He rose from the chair. Some things were best done standing, he thought. Like refereeing. He saw this one coming. "Like a paramedic, Ma. Or a policeman. Melissa Ryan—" he nodded in Melissa's direction "—this, as you may or may not have already guessed, is my mother, Gina Santini, otherwise known as the Mom Squad."

"Your mother?" Melissa repeated. The woman looked too young to be Del's mother. Looking closer, Melissa decided that he resembled his mother a great deal, as did Kathleen.

Gina rose, moving back her chair. Del watched her quickly size up the other woman and saw that whatever feelings she had as a protective mother, which she always loudly claimed were wasted on Del, melted at the sight of the delicate-looking young woman and the child before her. This was no hardened hussy who'd set her cap to trap her beloved son. This was a woman who'd been hurt, and very recently.

She approached Melissa and peered at the baby in her arms. Della was squirming and making noise, but it wasn't a whimper yet. Gina raised her eyebrows, softening immediately. "May I hold her?"

Del grinned. Two minutes before, his mother had been the indignant inquisitor. Now she was all oohs and aahs, reduced to mush over the sight of a baby. It ran in the family, he thought ruefully. He crossed his arms and leaned back against the counter, content to watch his mother in action.

Melissa surrendered her daughter into Gina's arms, albeit reluctantly. "Yes, of course."

Gina was quick to take Della. The feel of the brand-new baby had her eyes fluttering closed as she absorbed the sheer pleasure of it. Della began to fuss.

"Hush, hush, little one. Here, lots of room for you to place your head," she murmured to Della as she pressed the tiny head against her own breast.

Melissa watched the older woman intently, and when she looked up they shared a smile. Every mother knew no one could hold her baby right but her.

Gina nodded at the pizza. "Why don't you two eat your dinner before it gets cold? My brother-in-law's not too bright, but he knows how to make exquisite pizza." She kissed her fingertips and then released them in a quick motion, just the way the flavor exploded on the palate after tasting one of Fazio's meals. "Come, we'll get acquainted, little one."

Melissa watched as the woman disappeared into the other room, softly crooning the same song she'd heard Del singing to Della in the wee hour of the morning. Except that Gina's voice was beautiful. "Does everyone in your family just take charge like that?"

"We're Italian. It's in the blood." He subtly moved the pizza closer to her. "Sometimes, though, it's a struggle to maintain an identity."

She could relate to that. She was having trouble finding hers.

Melissa sat at the table again. It would be so very easy to get swept away by these people and let everyone else do for her as she healed at her leisure. Kathleen and Gina certainly seemed eager to help. And of course, there was Del.

But that would be a mistake. *Tomorrow* sounded seductive, so much better than *today*. But it was today that she had to reconstruct, to seize, if she was ever to be her own person. If she was never going to be hurt again.

She looked off toward the other room. Gina's voice floated back to her. It was a voice made for lullabies. "Anyone ever get lost in the power struggle?"

He thought of his brothers and sister. They were all their own people. "Not a one." He picked up a soda from the table, opened it and began to take a drink, but then remembered his manners. He poured two glasses. "Ma knows when to back off, though it's usually only temporary."

She accepted the glass he moved in her direction. "Same as you."

He grinned above his glass. "Same as me. Like I said, it's in the blood."

She looked at him meaningfully. "I want my own identity, too."

"Admirable."

She finished her slice, then wondered if she had room inside for more. The pizza was still hot and tempting. "That's something I forgot for a while, being with—"

"Your husband." Though he didn't mean to, Del bit the word off. To cover the slip, he placed another slice on her plate and avoided her eyes.

"Alan," Melissa said.

It was a sin of omission, she told herself. She didn't correct him, she just let him assume that she was supplying Alan's name rather than substituting it for the title.

Coward, a small voice echoed within her.

"I got so caught up in living a dream that I forgot to hold on to me. Until he took it all."

"Not all," Del disputed. Didn't she see that? There was still a good deal of her left. She just had to realize it. "There's a lot left. It'll just take you a little while to get it all together."

He was crowding her, he thought. He could see it in her expression. Casually he backed off, taking a third slice. "But you can take all the time you want. I like having a clean house."

Melissa's tense expression softened into a smile.

As if on cue, Gina returned, sans baby. "She's

asleep," she said in answer to Melissa's unspoken question.

Gina's own expressive face registered surprised disbelief. "What have you done to this house?" she asked Del. "There are fresh towels in the bathroom and no dust anywhere." She turned to Melissa, knowing it was her doing all along. "You did this, didn't you?"

"Well, I—" Melissa didn't know whether to admit it, or take her pizza slice and flee. No, she was through fading into the background. "Yes, I did."

Gina looked at Del. "You let her get away and you are a bigger fool than your Uncle Antonio was."

Melissa looked to Del for an explanation. "Uncle Tony never married. He enjoyed—" Del paused for a second as he tried to find the right word that would put a more delicate spin on the concept. "Variety."

"Now the old goat is enjoying being alone in his last years." Gina took a seat next to Melissa. There was no beating around the bush for her. "You like my son?"

Del almost choked on his slice. "Ma!"

Gina waved a hand to silence him. "He's a lot of trouble, I grant you. A *lot* of trouble. But then, he was a breech baby. I should have known then he'd be trouble. The others were born one, two, three." She snapped her fingers in quick succession to punctuate her words. "But not him, not Delveccio."

Melissa stared at him. "That's your real name?"

He had always hated it. "I don't advertise it much.

Ma handles that end of it.'' He looked at the small woman now. ''Back off, Ma.''

''Hey, is that the way to talk to your mother?''

''It is if she's crowding my guest.'' He emphasized the last word and hoped it would assuage any of Melissa's fears that his mother's words had raised. ''My mother was born with this matchmaking instinct. If it was up to her, we would have all been betrothed at birth.''

Gina didn't bother to argue. ''It would have been easier.''

''I'm sorry about this, Melissa.'' And she could see that he really was. ''Ma, she's married.''

Melissa winced. Each time the lie surfaced, it chafed that much more, made her feel that much more guilty. But now that she had him believing she was married, it was an impossible situation to rectify. What was she going to say, I lied because I didn't trust you? How could she pay him back like that?

Melissa saw Gina looking at her hand, staring at the very cheap gold-plated band on her left hand. Melissa could almost see Gina thinking that although it was the proper hand, something just wasn't right. She could smell it. If Melissa was married, what was she doing staying here?

Gina leaned forward, her hand covering Melissa's. Melissa could almost cry for the comfort she found there. ''Where is your husband, dear?''

There were times his mother came on like gangbusters. This was not the time or place. ''Ma, Kathy's probably calling you right now. The kids need a baby-sitter. She and Dennis haven't been out all month."

Gina acted as if she hadn't heard him. Melissa held Gina's gaze, knowing that there was something in her eyes, something that Gina could read and yet not fully understand. For a moment longer, Gina kept her hand over Melissa's, and then patted it.

"You call me if you have any trouble, eh? Del knows the number." She looked at her son and then shrugged. "Maybe." She rose to her feet. "And you, next time you need something—" she poked a stern finger in the center of his chest "—call me first."

Del took her arm and purposely guided her to the front door. "Why? I like leaving my lectures for last."

She took his face in her hands, though she had to stand on her toes to do it. "You be good to that girl, Del. She hurts."

He placed his hands over hers, a communion of spirit that made words secondary. "I know, Ma."

"You know why?"

He thought of the record collection Melissa insisted on carrying with her, the bits and pieces of conversation she'd let drop. "I've got my suspicions, but I'm not completely sure."

"It has to do with that husband of hers." Gina frowned. "Where is he?"

Del shook his head. "I don't know. He just abandoned her."

Gina muttered a few choice words in Italian, aptly describing a man who could do something like that to his wife and child. She stepped outside and then turned to face her son. "See if you can find him."

It wasn't what he expected her to ask. "What?"

Her eyes narrowed. "And then shoot him." She touched his cheek lightly. "I want her for you."

It wasn't just a whimsical request by a mother who wanted to see her son married. Del knew the difference. He heard it in her voice. She knew. "You can tell?"

"Yes." She nodded solemnly.

"Just like that?" he teased. He had to admit that this was a little too heavy for him. A little too scary, even though he wanted it.

"Just like that." Gina grinned, and the years melted away to nothing. She was twenty again. "It's a gift. Mothers of hell-raisers get it. It is called compendition."

"Compensation," he corrected patiently.

She glided right over the correction to the heart of the matter. "You've heard of it."

"No, just of you. See you, Ma." He kissed her cheek and closed the door behind her. He could understand why his father had been crazy about her until the day he died. Gina Santini was something else.

Melissa ventured into the living room, having heard the door close. She'd waited, sensing that Gina had wanted some time alone with her son. "Is she gone?"

He turned from the door and laughed. "Yes, you can come out of the storm shelter now."

But she hadn't been hiding from Gina. She had found herself wishing that the woman had been her mother as well. While she was growing up, she could have done with the kind of concern she saw in Gina's bright green eyes. Things might have turned out differently for her. "Is that what's known as a whirling dervish?"

"I think my mother posed for the prototype. Don't let her get to you."

"It's okay." She smiled warmly. "I like her fussing. It was kind of nice."

"Didn't anyone ever fuss around you like that? I mean, I know not exactly like that. No one ever carried on the way Ma does, but—"

"No."

The single word, isolated and alone, cut through everything. The image of a young girl, left to her own devices, returned. Probably grew up neglected by her parents and then abandoned by her husband. Not much of a track record for the human race to go on. No wonder she didn't trust people easily. Del was determined to change the odds around for her.

"I'll call her back." He pretended to open the door. "She can fuss over you to your heart's content."

Melissa grinned. He was being silly, but she liked it. She couldn't quite remember when she'd felt light enough to be silly. "No, I think I've had enough for one day."

He nodded gravely. "That's what we all say."

She walked in front of him to the kitchen. "Tell me about the others."

"What others?"

"Well, I've met Kathleen and I know that Drew

moved out last year to get married. What are the names of your other brothers?''

She sounded hungry to know. Did she have any siblings? No, something told him that she didn't. "There's Joe and Tony and Nick.''

She tucked the remainder of the pie back into the box. "Who's the oldest one?''

"Nick. But I'm taller.'' He flashed a grin. There'd always been that sense of friendly competition between him and Nick. In high school, it'd been almost intense. But as they grew older and their tastes likened, it had turned out all right. They would have gladly fought the world for each other. It went without saying. Talking about it would have only embarrassed both of them.

He saw that she was definitely finished and had reverted into the cleaning mode. "C'mon.'' He took her wrist, trying to draw her away from the sink. "I'll tell you all about them in the living room over a little red wine I've been saving.''

She didn't budge. "But the dishes—'' She'd grown up husbanding everything, putting everything back neatly into its place. It lasted longer that way. And there'd been so very little.

"—aren't planning on going anywhere,'' he finished for her. If it was stubborn she wanted, she'd met her match, he thought. Firmly he guided her toward the living room. As they passed Della's partially opened door, no whimpers or cries floated out to detain them. Del kept navigating.

"You've done enough cleaning in one day to merit getting into the housekeeping hall of fame."

It had been a monumental task. "I am kind of tired," she admitted. "And my feet hurt." They still felt a little puffy to her. She wondered when they would be back to normal. For that matter, she wondered when she would be back to normal.

"I'm surprised you're not totally wiped out. Just looking at all you've done makes me tired."

He pointed her to the swivel rocker rather than the sofa, and she sank into it gratefully. "Put your feet up," he coaxed, nudging the hassock over toward her.

She did and it felt wonderful. Her eyes began to flutter closed, then flew open again. She stared at him. "What are you doing?"

He had sat on the hassock and had one of her feet resting on his thigh. He was kneading her instep. "Massaging your foot."

She tried to pull it back, but he held her foot firmly captive. She swallowed, telling herself that it was absolutely ridiculous to have her bones feel as if they were being reduced to slush just because a man was running his fingers up and down her foot. "Why?"

"Because you said they hurt. Kathleen used to complain about her legs cramping and her feet hurting right after she had Erin." He felt the tension leave her, saw her stop clutching the arms of the chair. There was hope yet. "Feel good?"

It did. It felt wonderful. "Too good."

"I'll try not to be so good at it," he promised. He turned his attention to the other foot. She had small feet. Everything about her was small and delicate. He longed to show her just how precious she was. "Although there have been women who have wanted to marry me for my hands."

Their eyes met.

She wouldn't doubt it. And it wasn't just because of what he could do for leg cramps. She was sure, without ever having known it, that his touch was light and gentle and created whirlpools of desire within a woman.

Within her.

Look what he could do with just his eyes.

What was wrong with her? She'd just had a baby. Just been abandoned. And here she was, having thoughts, desires, needs. Was she crazy?

Yes, she probably was. But she didn't have the strength to resist.

Del had no idea how he had managed to move from her foot to her lips, but he had. One moment he was just looking up at her, his fingers carefully working her toes. The next moment his mouth was a hairbreadth away from hers, drawn there as if he had no will, no say of his own.

And in truth, he didn't.

Chapter Nine

His fingertips sensitized her skin as he gently framed her face in his hands. His lips whispered against hers, offering an unspoken promise she wanted desperately to believe and just as desperately to ignore.

Because it was too good to be true.

"Kiss me, Melissa." His mouth teased hers, gliding over the corners, making just the lightest of contacts. It made the ache that much more acute. "Kiss me back."

"Del." Anguish tore at her. "I can't."

But she already was.

She was lost and floating in the world his kiss created for her as it blotted out everything else. Her past, lessons learned. Everything. She moaned from the sheer pleasure of it, from the sheer anticipation of what was to come.

She was believing again, damn it, and sinking so

fast she couldn't even catch her breath. She grasped his shoulders, wanting to make contact with something real, something she could anchor herself to. With all her might, she wanted to push him away. Instead she clung, her fingers twisting into his shirt, wrinkling, crumbling, pulling.

It didn't set her free. It only served to bind her to him.

He couldn't begin to tell himself that he understood what was happening to him. Not any of it. He'd always had a weak spot for anyone who needed help, like his father before him. That was what had made him take her into his home. What made him take her into his heart was another matter entirely.

He really didn't want a woman and infant cluttering up his life. He liked his life just the way it was. At least he had thought he did. Until he had met her.

He couldn't think. He couldn't feel anything beyond the sensations that the touch of her mouth was generating within him. There was no life, no air, no world beyond the boundaries of this room, this woman.

He pulled her closer to him, one hand caressing the planes of her back. He had to touch her, needed to touch her, to absorb her softness. He needed it as much as he needed to wake up each morning. Slowly his hand crept up to her waist almost of its own volition. And then hesitantly, he moved his palms against her breasts, giving her ample opportunity to say no, praying she wouldn't.

She had to make him stop, yet no words formed.

None rose to her lips. The gentleness of his touch overwhelmed her. He was touching her as if she were a precious object. It made her want to cry. She moaned again, her kisses growing more fevered, her body fluid against his.

He couldn't be doing this, shouldn't be doing this. There were things to consider, things in the way. She had just given birth to another man's child.

With almost superhuman effort, he pulled himself free. Softly he kissed each eyelid and then held her close against his chest. "See, doesn't that relieve the cramps in your legs?" He couldn't believe that his voice wasn't trembling. Everything else within him was.

He was trying to lighten the situation. She was grateful, though a part of her wanted to reach out for more, for everything he had to give. "This is what you did for your sister?"

A soft chuckle rippled through his chest. She felt it against her cheek. Warmth and contentment filled her.

"No, you got the deluxe treatment. On the house." He heard Della crying in the background. Just as well. It would give him something to do and perhaps dim the yearning he felt. But he doubted it. "I think the princess is up again. My mother's lullabies used to be good for longer reprieves than that." He shrugged, rising, needing to put distance between them. "I guess memory has a way of coloring things."

"Yes," she agreed sadly. "It does." And hers were vividly colored. Each small kernel of hope had always had a major disappointment following in its wake. "I'd better see what she wants."

"No, let me." He resisted the temptation to press a hand on her shoulder. Right now, it was best not to touch her in any way. He wasn't certain just how much he could safely endure.

"But I—"

"Can do those dishes you were so attached to. I want to see my girl." He turned and left the room, moving quickly.

His girl. As if he were Della's father. Melissa watched him walk out. What if it had been different? What if he—

But it wasn't different. And it wasn't Del who had fathered her child, who had whispered words of love to her that were forgotten as soon as they were uttered.

She smiled ruefully to herself. Del was different. And maybe Del wouldn't disappoint her today, or tomorrow. But he would, by and by. It would come. If she let it.

Only, she told herself, walking into the kitchen, she wouldn't let it.

Easier said than done. With a sigh, she turned on the faucet. Melissa yelped as the hot water nipped her fingers. She adjusted the temperature quickly. Served her right for not paying attention. Next time, she swore, looking over her shoulder in the general direction of Della's room, she'd be alert.

"Hey, you look a little sleepy-eyed there, Officer Santini. How's it going?" Larry clamped a large,

hammy hand on Del's shoulder as he came up to him
in the precinct hallway.

Del wrinkled his nose. Bertha, the cleaning woman
who was as much a fixture in the precinct as the stone
steps leading up to the front entrance, had just waxed
the floors in this part of the corridor. She always used
too much. He hated the smell of wax.

"Okay." The one-word answer sounded a lot more
weary than he had meant it to. Three weeks' lack of
sleep was catching up to him.

"Still have that houseguest?" The grin on Larry's
face was wide.

Del could see that Larry thought there was a very
enviable reason for the tired look on his face.
"Guests," he corrected. "They come in two sizes.
The small, economy size has lungs that could have
outdone Ethel Merman in her heyday."

The interested grin faded. "If you say so. How's
the other one doing?"

Del thought of Melissa as she had been when he'd
left her this morning. They had slipped into a routine
that was both comforting and yet stimulating. There
was color in her cheeks and the beginning of liveli-
ness in her eyes. She laughed more easily now. And
only looked wary whenever their hands accidentally
touched, or their bodies brushed against each other by
the crib. He hadn't kissed her since that night on the
hassock. Fear had stopped him. Fear of pushing her
away, fear of reeling himself further in.

But the standoff couldn't last forever.

"She's coming along. She's trying to repay my hospitality by cleaning the house. I can't find a damn thing without a road map anymore." The only thing she hadn't touched was his service revolver, and that only because he had warned her not to. Otherwise it undoubtedly would be wearing a new coat of polish.

Larry could only laugh. "Any news on that husband of hers?"

Del shook his head. "None." And for his money, the bastard could stay lost. But his existence did complicate matters. A lot. Wanting her the way he did went against everything he believed in. He wasn't after a quick affair. He was after a relationship. Having to contend with a deserting husband really impeded the situation. Yet he couldn't help himself.

They stopped by the candy machine. Larry could never pass one by without feeding it money. And feeding himself. "Funny thing, life." He tossed two quarters into the slot. They musically announced their passage downward. "A lot of guys I know are looking for a woman just like that, and that no-good son of a gun runs out on her." He punched a number and a candy bar plopped down. He yanked it out. "Lucky for you he did, eh?"

"Yeah, lucky." He wasn't entirely certain about that, Del thought. If she hadn't happened into his life, he wouldn't be agonizing over things now. Life would be a lot more peaceful.

And a lot duller.

Larry bit into the candy bar, then looked at Del thoughtfully. "I'd get some sleep, if I were you, Del.

You're beginning to sound like a zombie.'' He left Del standing in the hall.

A zombie. Yes, maybe he did look and sound like one. But he knew it wasn't staying up long hours with Della that was turning him into one. Not if he was being honest with himself.

Melissa looked at Del. He was sitting across from her at the kitchen table, and he looked as if he was going to fall asleep right in the middle of his mashed potatoes, despite the lively music coming from the radio she always kept on. His eyes were a bit droopy from lack of sleep, yet it only made him appear sexy to her. Everything made him look sexy. And that was the trouble. Her feelings for him were growing and tangling her up inside. She was going to have to leave soon, she told herself. She had imposed on him enough as it was. And if she didn't go soon, she'd never be able to make herself leave. Until he sent her away, or something else equally drastic happened.

"I'm sorry."

Del looked up at her quizzically, puzzled by her apology.

"She kept you up again last night, didn't she?"

He waved away her words, then pushed aside the plate. He was too tired to really eat. "I couldn't sleep, anyway. Too much on my mind."

"Police work?"

"In a way." He saw her interest rise at his vague response. "Investigative stuff."

That didn't exactly sound very professional. She

was finished and she rose, taking his plate with hers. "Can you talk about it?"

"Yeah."

Melissa turned, waiting for him to go on. She wanted to share in his life. As a friend, she insisted to herself. After all, he'd come through for her when she'd had no one.

"What color do you like?"

She stared at him. "What?"

Del scraped the chair along the floor and tilted it back slightly. Suddenly he didn't feel tired anymore. He must have gotten a second wind. "Am I slurring?" He laced his hands behind his neck. "I don't feel like I'm slurring, but then, I don't think I look as tired as everyone keeps telling me I look."

She reached under the sink for the bottle of dishwashing liquid and squirted it into the running water. "No, you're not slurring, but what does my favorite color have to do with your investigative work?"

He raised his voice to be heard above the tap water. "I'm trying to investigate you." Her shoulders stiffened. She was shying away again. He hadn't gained as much ground in three weeks as he'd hoped. It was time for some of the blanks to be filled in. "You know, I don't know that much about you. I mean, I know all I need to know, in my head, but it would be nice to fill in some of the gaps."

She stared at the soap bubbles as they multiplied beneath her fingers, dancing away from the force of the water coming from the faucet. "Blue."

He leaned forward in his chair, still looking at the

back of her head. But if he came any closer, he was afraid she would shy away again. "What?"

"My favorite color is blue."

He smiled to himself. "Where were you born?"

Melissa licked her lips. This was a mistake. The less he knew, the better. "I don't think—"

He rose, coming to her side. "Hey, we're on a roll here, don't stop now."

The comical look on his face had her relenting. What harm would it do, really? "Georgia."

He picked up a towel and mechanically wiped the dish she put in the rack. It didn't occur to him that he never dried dishes. "It's a big state. Could you narrow it down just a little?"

"Outside of Savannah." She remembered what it had looked like. The way the carnations had smelled. "Way outside."

Yes, they were definitely on a roll here. "Any brothers or sisters?" Though he thought he already knew the answer to that, there was no harm in verifying it.

"None that I know of." And she had wanted them desperately. To have someone to talk to. Someone to love who would love her back.

Her answer took him aback for a moment. Was she being flippant? No, that wasn't really like her. He realized that Melissa had never mentioned anything about her mother or father. Was she an orphan? "Have I put my foot in my mouth again?"

"Why?" She couldn't help grinning. He was so sensitive of her feelings. She'd never met anyone like

him before. "Do you taste shoe leather, Santini?"
When he started to answer, she shook her head. She
owed him a few answers in return for his hospitality.
And her past didn't really matter that much. Not anymore. Not if she didn't let it. "My father left us when
I was about seven or eight." A rueful smile traced
the corners of her lips. "The pack-of-cigarettes bit."

Just like her husband. Del could have kicked himself for bringing this up.

"My mother sort of went to pieces after that. She
blamed everything for his walking out on us. She
blamed it on the fact that he was out of work. On
me—"

"You?" He was stunned. How could anyone
blame a child for their husband leaving?

"Yes," Melissa replied sadly. It had seemed simple enough to her then. "He didn't want to be tied
down, and a kid meant the ultimate in responsibility.
She blamed everything and everyone, but mostly, I
think she blamed herself. She drank a lot after that.
Stayed out nights." Melissa tried to keep the shiver
away, but it came, just as surely as the memory did.
"Sometimes she didn't come home at all."

He had stopped drying, the towel hanging from his
fingers. Now he knew what he was up against. "So
you've been dealing with being abandoned ever since
you were young." And it was up to him to turn a
lifetime pattern around for her. He had picked easier
tasks for himself, but none more important.

Melissa flushed. She kept her eyes on the bubbles

in the sink. "How did we get to this? I thought I was apologizing about Della keeping you up."

"And I wound up telling you how much I wanted to know about you. It's called having a conversation, Melissa."

She didn't have as much strength of character as she had thought she did. She kept slipping backward. This need to make contact kept engulfing her. Melissa rinsed a bowl and placed it on the rack a little too firmly. "The less you know, the better."

"I've never found that to be true." He wanted to ask more, reassure more, but it was still too soon. Some things you couldn't rush, no matter how much you wanted to. "Remember Disneyland?"

Boy, when he switched gears, he really switched them. "Funny place in the middle of Anaheim? Has a castle?" Relieved that he wasn't going to ask any more probing questions, she could play along with this.

"That's the place." Carelessly he flung the towel onto the hook she'd fastened just for that purpose. It missed and fell to the floor. He didn't notice. "I told you I was taking Kathy's kids at the end of the month. Well, tomorrow is the end of the month."

She stooped to pick up the towel and hung it up properly. "You read calendars very well."

"The invitation is still open."

"I don't think it's a good idea." For a hundred different reasons, she thought.

He cornered her by the refrigerator as she tried to

move aside. "You're outvoted. I think it's a great idea."

She lifted a brow. "That makes it one to one."

"Della votes with me." His eyes teased her, brushing along her mouth for just the barest moment. She felt her heart begin to quicken. "Kathleen's coming along to help us herd everyone."

"But—"

His hands were on either side of her, bracketing any avenue of escape until she said yes. "My treat."

Melissa closed her eyes for a second, gathering strength. She felt herself weakening even as she tried to be strong. Maybe it would be fun at that. "Don't you accept the word no?"

He grinned. "Never heard of it."

Maybe if she tried to put it another way. "Del, you've been incredibly sweet." She never got a chance to say the word "but."

"Lady, haven't you heard? I'm the flavor of the month."

Yes, she thought, the flavor of the month. And next month, after she moved out, it would be over and she'd be left with a taste on her tongue and a yearning that she had no way to fulfill.

Del wanted to kiss her, to find that wild, exhilarating place he always seemed to stumble into whenever his lips touched hers. Instead he took her hands in his. "I'm not taking no for an answer. It's time you got out of here, away from the cleanser and took in some fresh air for a change. You've been here over three weeks and I haven't taken you anywhere."

"Like dancing."

He liked the sudden flash of mischief in her eyes. He saw it all too infrequently. "What?"

She grinned. She was being silly again. He did that to her. "It sounded like one of those sit-com situations where the wife complains to her husband that he hasn't taken her dancing."

"You want dancing?"

There was a look in his eyes she couldn't quite fathom. What was he up to? "No, I didn't mean—"

But it was too late. Leaving one hand tucked around hers, he placed the other in the small of her back. It felt deliciously intimate. In the background, a group from the fifties was crooning about their girl on the oldies station. The music was soft and dreamy. And perfect. Del swayed in time, moving with grace that, somehow, didn't surprise her.

"Any other requests that you'd like filled?" His breath caressed her cheek even as it jump-started her heart.

"I'm afraid to ask." She laughed, feeling incredibly giddy. He made her want to laugh, to reach up and catch sunbeams. He made her forget it wasn't possible.

His eyes darkened just a little as he looked into hers, wishing that she'd trust him. Wishing he'd met her before life had hurt her so badly. "Never be afraid of anything, Melissa."

But she knew better.

Melissa clung to him as they bumped and barreled into darkness on the roller-coaster ride. Outside, Kathleen stood bathed in sunlight, four children of various sizes gathered around her as she waited for Del and Melissa to return. She had insisted Melissa go on this ride almost as much as Del had.

A shriek burst almost involuntarily from Melissa's lips as they plunged down, followed by laughter. The sound reminded Del of a delighted child, the child she'd never been allowed to be. Del was glad he had bullied her into coming. This morning, just as they were about to leave, she had tried to back out. He hadn't let her. The trip would be good for her, he insisted. And for the baby. They both needed it.

When she complained about getting sunburned, he produced suntan lotion. When she said that she had nothing to carry Della in, he produced a carryall and a stroller, courtesy of Kathleen.

All her protests fell on deaf ears. So she went.

And had a ball.

"Smile," he ordered as he suddenly whirled on her, a camera where his face should be.

They were standing in line for one of the more picturesque, tamer rides in Fantasyland that all the children could enjoy. She heard the click. It was too late to throw her hands in front of her face. "You're wasting all your film on me," she protested.

A whirling noise told him that the camera was rewinding itself. Time for more film. He dug another roll out of his shirt pocket and waited for the camera to be silent. "Taking photographs is never a waste. I like memories." He had already gone through two rolls and they'd only been at the park for three hours.

"You have pictures?" She watched him carefully extract his film, then reload his camera.

"Shoe boxes full," Kathleen chimed in as she grabbed Stevie before he could run to attack an unsuspecting Donald Duck.

Melissa looked at Del. She could easily envision it. He probably tossed packs of photographs into shoe boxes the way he tossed everything else. "Really? Shoe boxes?"

He heard the inflection in her voice. "Uh-oh. I smell another project coming on." Erin tugged on his jeans, raising her arms to him. Wordlessly, as if all this was second nature to him, Del picked her up. He brushed a hand along her back as she rested her head on his shoulder. His eyes never left Melissa's face.

Melissa flushed. He was getting too good at second-guessing the way her mind worked. She shrugged. "I'd do it, but I don't know your family. I couldn't arrange the photographs chronologically."

The idea of her poring through his family's photographs, arranging them into albums, appealed to him. "Easy enough to remedy. Kath?"

"I could lend you our albums," Kathleen offered. "It would make it simpler if you really wanted to undertake the job. But you don't know what you'd be getting yourself into."

Wrong, Melissa thought. She knew all too well. Quicksand. She was getting into quicksand. She stepped further into it each time she got a little more involved in Del's life. Each time she let him get a little more involved in hers. And when it swallowed her up whole, there'd be nothing left. Nothing to pull together when he was gone.

"I can handle it," she said firmly, trying to vanquish her own ghosts.

Del had a feeling she was saying that in answer to something else, but he pretended not to notice. "I'm sure that there isn't very much you can't handle."

Their eyes met and held as the young girl in the pirate costume gestured them in to the next flying pirate ship.

It was all fantasy, Melissa told herself, sitting down. The guardrail snapped shut, holding her, Erin, Della and Del in place.

Fantasy. But for now, just for now, she'd pretend to believe. Pretending was all right as long as she remembered that it *was* just pretend.

Chapter Ten

Del tucked the bottle of champagne under his arm as he turned the key and unlocked his front door. Walking in, he stood a moment as the light fragrance of her perfume wafted around him. He loved the scent she wore. Delicate and airy, it teased his senses and excited him the moment he caught a whiff of it. He had to concentrate in order to detect it. It was almost imperceptible, but it was there. He only needed to stop and notice it. Just like her influence on his life.

After helping his mother raise his younger brothers and sister, he had been certain that the responsibilities of married life weren't meant for him. He wanted to be footloose, to be free. There were more than enough family ties for him to deal with as it was. He wasn't lacking for involvement, and he didn't need to become entrenched in any further relationships. He certainly hadn't had any plans to.

Until Melissa had zipped into his life in that battered silver bullet she called a van.

Things just seemed to fall into place then without any effort or real thought on his part. They fell into place as if they had always meant to fit exactly that way. He liked the order she had brought into his life, both physically and mentally. She'd focused him, brought his energy to play in just one area instead of being scattered in various directions. The relationships he'd had with women up to now had all been rather aimless, nomadic. He enjoyed their company, but there had been no spark, excitement. Not like there was every time he was with her. It was Melissa who made him look in a different light at the responsibility attached to having a family. She made it look enticing, satisfying. She had focused him because now he knew exactly what he wanted out of life.

For the first time in his life, he liked the idea of having a family of his own.

This family.

Maybe tonight, after they'd celebrated a little, he could get her to talk about setting the wheels in motion for divorcing her husband. He wanted to marry her. He wanted her to be his alone and for Della to be his daughter, not someone else's.

"Hi!" It felt good to sing out a greeting, knowing she was around somewhere to answer. He pulled his key out of the lock and pocketed it, closing the door behind him. He grasped the bottle in his hand again. "I'm home."

Melissa was in the kitchen. The sound of his voice

brought a tingle of anticipation, of excitement to her, the way it always seemed to every time he walked into the house. Into her life.

Stop it, she thought. *Get hold of yourself. This is temporary, just temporary, remember?*

"Hi." She wiped her hands on the dish towel she had casually draped over one shoulder as she walked into the living room.

The pull was instantaneous, as soon as he saw her. How could anyone in cutoff jeans and a checkered shirt tied at the waist look so completely delectable? She was barefoot as she stood in front of him. He had visions of her being barefoot up to her lovely neck, her sweet body pressed against his.

He realized he was squeezing the neck of the bottle and loosened his hold.

Melissa looked at the bottle quizzically. "What's that for?"

"We're celebrating."

He sounded mysterious as he placed his hand on the small of her back and guided her to the kitchen. "You've got your man?" she guessed when he didn't elaborate.

Maybe they'd skip dinner altogether, he mused, and just get to the celebrating part right away. He liked the thought of that. He'd show her just how she should be treated, how she should be loved.

"No, Mounties do that. We just get to read them their rights." He raised the bottle slightly. "This is to celebrate Della sleeping through the night."

She reached into the overhead cabinet and took out two wineglasses. "You noticed."

When Melissa had woken this morning and looked at the clock, she had hurried into Della's room, certain that something had to be wrong because the baby hadn't cried all night. But Della was fine, just on the verge of loudly proclaiming her hunger.

"Every blissful, quiet moment." He resisted the temptation of slipping his arm around her waist and pulling her to him, absorbing her softness. He knew he could have stayed that way forever. Del Santini, voted Mr. Suave in high school, head over heels and drooling over a barefoot woman. "You don't know what a big deal that is. Drew didn't sleep through the night until he was four years old."

She laughed as she placed the glasses on the table. He caught himself thinking how much he loved the sound of her laughter. How much it had brightened his life. "No, really." Giving in, he set the bottle on the table next to the glasses and slipped his arms around her. "We're also celebrating something else."

"What?" She didn't know what to expect. Part of her was wary, yet part tingled with anticipation. His enthusiasm was infectious.

"It's been four weeks since you've moved in."

He made it sound so permanent. She had to keep this all in perspective if she was going to make it on her own. Her smile faded slightly. "I've been meaning to talk to you about that."

She must have been the most honest woman he'd ever known. "Don't start in on how you want to pay

me back. You've cleaned enough things in here to
live rent-free for the rest of your life.''

"Del—''

There was a catch in her voice. He felt himself
tensing, waiting for a blow to land. Was she going to
tell him that her husband had turned up? That she
was going to go away with him? He hadn't realized
until this moment that he had been waiting for this to
happen. Dreading this would happen. He kept his
smile in place, but it felt as if it was cracking around
the edges.

"What?''

She glanced at the newspaper she had left neatly
folded on the side of the counter. She had it turned
to the classifieds. "I think I found a job.''

He could have kissed her, the relief that flooded
through his veins was that overwhelming. "Isn't it a
little soon? You only had the baby a month ago.''

Gently she eased herself out of his arms. He could
arouse her with just a look, a smile. Being there was
far too dangerous. She had to keep her mind on the
course she was setting for herself. "Farm women
used to have babies in the morning and go back to
work in the afternoon.''

He removed the foil from the bottle and began
working the cork loose. "Last time I looked, the north
forty didn't need plowing.'' The cork exploded out of
the bottle, shooting up to the ceiling before landing
on the floor. It rolled under the table.

Melissa ducked under it and picked up the cork as

he filled the glasses. "I need to go to work, Del. I need to feel independent again."

He could understand that. Independence had always seemed like a precious commodity to him. But it was only when he gained it that he realized he didn't feel threatened by the fact that at times he was interdependent as well. How long before she came to that conclusion? *Would* she come to that conclusion?

"Fine." He handed her a glass. "I just don't want you rushing into anything because you feel you have to. There's no hurry. I'm not planning to evict you."

I'm planning to marry you, he added silently, *when the time is right.*

"The job might be filled if I wait too long."

"What is it?" It occurred to him that he didn't even know what it was she did for a living. She hadn't mentioned it. Hadn't really mentioned very much that he hadn't forcibly dragged out of her.

"A teaching position. At a private kindergarten." Melissa took the paper from the counter and showed him the ad.

He saw the excitement in her eyes. How could he stand in the way of something that made her look so happy? He took the ad from her and looked it over. "Knew it was a mistake leaving the paper lying around," he murmured dryly. But he grinned at her, letting her know that he was behind her decision.

She suddenly frowned as she took the ad back. "But I'm going to have to find a day-care center for Della." This was going to be the part she hated, leaving her baby with strangers. Having a stranger care for Della, seeing moments that she was entitled to see. But these were luxuries she couldn't afford. There was a living to be made. And a future to build.

He knew he could easily fuel the indecision he saw in her eyes. But that would be fighting dirty. If she wanted this, then he wanted it for her. "What about Kathleen?"

"To take care of Della?"

He nodded.

She shook her head. "I'm sure your sister would love to take care of another baby."

"No, really." He set his glass down, untouched. "She's involved in a baby co-op."

The timer went off behind her and she shut off the stove. Grabbing two pot holders, she took out of the oven the quiche lorraine she'd prepared. Turning, she set it on the table. "Baby co-op? Is that like rent-a-baby?"

He was surprised at the amount of trivia he'd picked up, just listening to Kathleen and the others in his family talk. He got a kick out of explaining it to Melissa. "No, a group of women get together and watch each other's children for a few hours a day. One lady gets all of them one day and so on."

She tried to picture it. At times Della was too much for her. And that was just one child. "Sounds overwhelming."

"Kathleen assures me she loves it. Especially when it's someone else's turn." He took the spatula that she handed him.

Melissa sat down, pulling the chair in after her. "But I wouldn't be able to take a turn—"

"No problem." He was determined to make this work for her, if this was what she wanted. Besides Kathleen adored Della. "You pay something instead. Supply treats for the kids or the coloring books or something."

She was doubtful, but it did seem like the perfect solution. She promised herself to call Kathleen the first chance she got tomorrow. Melissa liked Kathleen. She could trust her. And if Kathleen trusted these other mothers, then that seemed a lot better to her than leaving Della in some impersonal center where she might or might not get the proper care she needed.

Melissa cut a slice of the quiche for herself. "I'll talk to Kathleen."

"After we celebrate."

She'd started the ball rolling. She might as well tell him the rest. Maybe after she told him he wouldn't see the need to celebrate her being here a month. "Del—"

His fork hovered over his plate, his appetite suddenly waning. "There's more, isn't there?"

Why was there this bittersweet feeling? She'd been happy about her decision just before he arrived home. Now, somehow, the words were difficult to form. "I found an apartment."

He tried to keep his voice light. "What are you going to do with it?"

"Move in if I get the job."

He raised his eyes to her face. His own were expressionless. He worked hard at that. "Why?"

She gestured helplessly. "Because I can't stay here forever." *Even though I want to.*

He wanted to ask why again, but knew he couldn't. Leaving was her decision to make, and he couldn't railroad her into staying.

Maybe it was best she did move out. It would help him clear his head a little. Lately all he could think about was her. Each time he saw her, each time she was in the room, each time she materialized in his mind, his desire grew. He didn't know how much more he could take, seeing her and not having her.

But he didn't want her giving in to him out of a sense of gratitude or for any other reason than the one he felt. He wanted her to love him.

He pressed his fingers to his eyes. And there was still the matter of her husband. They couldn't very well go forward with any sort of a relationship until that was resolved once and for all. She could easily obtain a divorce on the grounds of desertion. But she hadn't mentioned anything about trying to get a divorce. Maybe she was still hanging on to the hope that her husband would return. Why else would she be so reluctant to get involved with him? He knew she cared.

They needed breathing space to sort things out.

He slid his finger along the side of the tall wineglass. "I guess we could use this to celebrate your new independence and getting on with your life."

"Yes, we could."

Why didn't it feel any better than this? she wondered. She was finally doing exactly what she wanted, and yet, there was this leaden feeling about it, as if she wanted him to protest, to tell her—

What? That he loved her? That he wanted her to stay here with him forever?

Yes, damn it, she wanted that, and knew at the same time that if it happened, she'd never regain her own identity, her own sense of self. She needed to stand alone.

She thought of Kathleen, of Gina and all the help she had gotten and would be needing with Della in the months ahead.

Well, she amended, to stand as alone as she could. Besides, she would pay everyone back, starting with Del. She watched him raise his glass in a toast and followed suit.

"To you. May you get everything you want," he said. *And may there be more than just a small spot in all that for me.*

He placed the glass down and tried to concentrate on eating. She did make a mean quiche. But he couldn't seem to rouse his appetite anymore. "You're going to need first and last month's rent and security," he pointed out, nibbling on the crust.

"If I get the job."

In his heart, he knew she would. If not this one, then the next. "No reason why you shouldn't. You have a teaching license, right?"

She chewed on her lower lip uncertainly. His gut

tightened as he found himself wanting to do the same. "For Georgia and Arizona."

Something else he didn't know about her. Another piece to fit into the complete portrait of Melissa he was constructing in his mind. She'd gone on to get an education apparently without help from either parent. It just proved to him how much of a fighter she was. But then, he already knew that.

"As far as I know, they speak the same language in California as they do in Georgia and Arizona. Getting teaching credentials shouldn't be that hard. Nick's wife, Krys taught in a private school before they got married. Teaching credentials weren't required there. They're not as picky about some points as public schools are." He leaned over and covered her hand. "You'll knock 'em dead."

She needed the kind of encouragement he had to give. The prospect of starting over did make her nervous. She thought of what he'd said. "I guess I could apply for a small loan—"

"What's your collateral?" It would be the first thing the bank would ask, and she had none. No collateral, no work record here. Nothing except for him. He saw her face cloud over. He hated to see her like that. "I'll lend you the money," he said quietly.

She couldn't keep taking from him. "No, you've done enough already—"

The woman was going to corner the market on pigheaded stubbornness. "I said I'll lend you the money. If this is what you want, then I'll help."

She smiled, knowing there was no way to talk him

out of it. The man was a born giver. "I'm going to be in debt to you for the rest of my life."

"Nothing wrong with that." He finished his champagne, then raised his eyes to her face. Since it was a time for upheavals, he had one of his own. "I've got a question for you."

"Yes?" She'd never seen him look so serious before.

Don't ask me to stay, she suddenly thought. *I want too much to stay and it would be wrong.*

"Don't you think it's about time you got a divorce?" He saw the look that entered her eyes, the wary one that told him she was backing away. This time, he didn't pay attention to it. "Look, I know you don't want to talk about it, but I do. You're starting a new life. Fine, terrific. But don't you think you should get rid of some of the excess baggage from your old one as well?"

He caught himself just in time. The anger he felt was seeping into his voice. There was no excuse for it. "Besides, some of us are old-fashioned. We don't relish having erotic, sexy fantasies about married women." His eyes grew dark, the way they did when he tried to control his desire and just barely accomplished it. "And I do. Very sexy fantasies."

She was trapped. "Del, I—"

He raised his hand. He didn't want to hear excuses from her. Couldn't she see her way clear here? "Maybe you think you still love him, but he left you, Melissa." He wanted to take her and shake some sense into her. He wanted to take her and make love with her so badly he had no idea how he was keeping his hands off her. "He doesn't even know what you gave birth to, a boy, a girl, Mighty Mouse—"

"Mighty Mouse?"

His mouth curved slightly. "I'm trying for humor here because if I don't, I'm liable to say things you don't seem to want to hear yet."

Guilt shot through her with wickedly pointed shafts. He was being so nice to her, trying so hard to think of her feelings. He was going to hate her when she told him that she'd been lying. But she couldn't stand it any longer, couldn't stand the fact that she had been lying to him all this time.

With a trembling hand, she placed her fingertips to his lips to keep him from going on.

She hesitated. Why was telling the truth the hardest thing she'd ever done? Because she was afraid he'd turn from her. But it had to be said.

"Del, I'm not married."

He stared at her for a long moment, trying to comprehend her words. "What?" He looked down at her hand. The ring was still there.

Melissa weighed her words carefully, afraid she'd cry. That wouldn't help anything. It never did.

She nervously turned the band on her finger. "I bought that myself. It—it eased my self-consciousness when all these old women would look at my round stomach and have these smug expressions on their faces like I was less of a person because I was having a baby out of wedlock. I lost my last job because of that. They said it was bad for the image of the school. I didn't want my baby born into a world that shunned her because of what her mother had done.''

She'd lied to him. He loved her and she had lied to him. The glaring fact cut through him like a razor.

He kept his voice calm, so calm that it frightened her. She would have rather have had him yell at her. ''Why didn't you tell me? Why did you let me go on like some kind of an idiot?''

She pressed her eyes closed, fighting to keep the hot tears back. If he yelled, she could have kept them at bay. But he wasn't yelling. He was hurting. She could see that. And she ached because of it. Because it was her fault. ''I thought it was a good way to keep us from getting involved.''

''Well, it didn't work, did it?''

He took her into his arms. He wanted to yell, to hurt her the way she had him. But hurt was at the root of all this, and there was to be no more hurting if he could prevent it.

Damn, why couldn't she trust him after he'd practically cut himself wide open for her? After he'd fallen in love with her?

Struggling, Del managed to hold on to his temper, his hurt, his desire. Taking a deep breath, he let it out slowly. ''You're pretty lousy at strategy, you know that, don't you?''

She looked into his eyes and saw myriad emotions she couldn't begin to untangle. They mirrored, she realized, exactly what was going on inside of her. ''I guess I am at that.''

It was all the admission he needed. "So, you're not married," he repeated, as if to reassure himself that this wasn't something he just dreamed up because he wanted it so badly.

"No."

"Well," he said slowly, "that'll save money on divorce proceedings." He gave her a wicked grin. Long ago he'd learned that grudges and hard feelings were counterproductive to life. And he meant to live the rest of his with her. "Nice to know I've been lusting after a single woman instead of a married one. Makes it a lot simpler."

"No, it doesn't." She strained to hear the sound of Della crying for her. But there was only the music from the radio. Where was childish interference when you really needed it?

"Why?"

She knew he'd press. She couldn't blame him after what she'd just told him. "Because."

He saw it all in her eyes. Just because she wasn't married to the guy didn't mean she hadn't been hurt by him. Ultimately it didn't change a damn thing. For her. For him it was another story.

But his story didn't count right now. Only hers did. Until she could come to terms with everything that had happened to her so far, he knew he hadn't a prayer of making their relationship work.

All he could do was go on, making things as easy for her as he could. And wait.

The quiche was cold, but he liked it better that way. "So, when is the interview?"

"I was going to call tomorrow."

"Great. I'll get Kathleen to come over with the tribe. She can watch Della for you while you're being interviewed." Her glass was only half-empty, but he refilled it for her, then did the same for his own, even though the taste had gone flat for him.

For a moment, Melissa watched the foam settle in the glass. "Del."

Was there more? He didn't think he could be reasonable about anything else. "Yes?"

"I'm sorry."

"For what?"

"For complicating your life. For not being able to be free to feel. For everything."

"Don't be. Just be happy." He sampled his own champagne and decided that perhaps it wasn't flat after all. He promised himself that one day she would be happy. And it would be with him.

"If I could love anyone," she began haltingly, then stopped. *If I could let myself love.* She licked her lips, forcing herself to finish. "It'd be you."

"Don't worry," he smiled, lifting his glass in another toast. "It will be."

If only she could believe that, she thought. For both their sakes.

Chapter Eleven

"Now it's not much," Melissa told Del nervously as she slipped her key into the lock of her new apartment. She kept telling herself that his approval shouldn't matter so much to her, but there was no denying that it did.

Della, safely strapped into her carryall against Melissa's chest, grabbed a fistful of her mother's hair and yanked, trying to pull it into her mouth. Melissa winced as she pulled herself free. "But I thought with a little paint and cleaning, it would be all right."

She had made the same comment when she first told him about the apartment. Just how bad was this place? Del wondered.

"Well, let's see," he urged. He was carrying Della's crib in one hand, her giant teddy bear in the other. He had dragged them from the parking lot and his arms were beginning to ache.

Taking a fortifying breath, Melissa pushed open the door and let him walk in first. She knew that he'd think it was bleak. It *was* bleak, but it was all she could afford for now. Later, when things were going better, when she was officially certified and could teach in the public school system, she'd look for a bigger apartment. And a newer one. For now, this was close to her job and not that far from Del and Kathleen. It suited her utilitarian purposes.

Del set down the bear Melissa had whimsically named Mr. Ted and opened up the crib for Della. Then he looked around. Slowly.

"I'd say with a lot of paint and cleaning." Why did she want to stay here when she could remain at his house? No, he'd promised himself not to go over that again. There was no point to it. This was the way she wanted things and this was the way they were going to be. For the time being.

He helped Melissa off with the harness, taking Della from her as she slipped the navy ties aside. His fingers brushed against Melissa's breasts as he pulled Della free of the leg holes. His skin tingled as he placed Della into the crib.

Clearing his throat, Del took three steps and was in the kitchen. "Hey, you have a refrigerator," he said in surprise.

Melissa double-checked that the crib locks were in place, then came up behind Del. "I'm renting it from the management."

The apartment looked roomy only because there was nothing in it beside the refrigerator and the crib.

"What are you doing for furniture?" It was a little late to ask, but he thought he should, just in case.

She shrugged, shoving her hands deep into her jeans. Furniture had been too expensive to rent by the month, although there was one furnished apartment vacant at the moment. "I can just use a sleeping bag for the time being. Della has a crib, thanks to you and Kathleen. That's all that really matters for now."

He lifted a brow. "Spartan quarters," he pronounced. "Going to eat off the floor?"

He wasn't helping any. She gestured toward the kitchen. "Maybe a card table."

Del moved over toward the small kitchen window. "How about a real table?"

That would have to be further along in the future. The first order of business would be getting a real bed. "In time."

He cracked the dark blinds and looked out on the parking lot. He saw the cars beginning to arrive. Lucky for everyone Melissa had rented a first-floor apartment, he thought. Nick's back wasn't what it used to be after moving that piano for Kathleen. "Three minutes sound about right to you?"

Melissa stared at him. What was he talking about? "Right for what?"

The doorbell rang in answer to her question, and Del turned to open it. The whole front of the apartment could be crossed in a little more than twenty steps. Melissa followed, curious. Who'd be ringing her doorbell? No one knew she was here, except for Del. Even when she had filled out the employment forms at the private school, she had used Del's address.

Del pushed the door as far back as it could go. Melissa's mouth dropped open. There were at least half a dozen people crowding in at her front door. Behind them were more people, trailing out into the parking bays that were directly beyond her apartment. People bearing furniture and boxes. Big ones.

She turned and looked at Del uncertainly. "Del?"

He grinned, taking a step back so as not to block the threshold. He pulled her along with him. "Melissa, I'd like you to meet the rest of my family."

"The rest of your family, or the rest of the state?" Melissa stood on her toes, trying to make an accurate head count. With the furniture and other things in the way, it was impossible. Every available space leading to her door was filled with either a body or a thing. "What is all this?"

Gina Santini pushed her way through the crowd she fed at her table on every occasion she could find an excuse for, making her way through the door. "You can't live in an empty place, Melissa." She patted the woman's face, smiling benevolently. "We have brought you things for your apartment."

Melissa knew they meant well, but this was charity, pure and simple. "I can't accept all this."

"Oh, please." The plea came from a blond-haired woman who had edged her way in behind Gina. She was clutching a very active-looking four-year-old by the hand. The little girl had jet-black hair, like Del. "You have no idea what a favor you're doing us."

The young woman vaguely waved a hand behind her. "This stuff has been in all our garages since forever. We need the extra room."

"That's Krys," Del interjected quickly before Melissa could ask. "She belongs to Nick." He pointed to a tall, dark-haired man toward the back of the line. Nick waved with his free hand. He was holding something with the other, but Melissa couldn't discern what it was. There was someone else in front of him.

"Actually, it's the other way around." Krys winked at Melissa. The girl she was hanging on to yanked impatiently on her arm.

"Momm-mmee."

Krys flashed an apologetic smile at Melissa. "Jennifer needs to use your bathroom. Where—" Krys looked around. "No, never mind." She waved Melissa back against Del. "I'll find it."

"Are they all like this?" Melissa whispered to Del. She looked over the faces in the crowd. There didn't seem to be a shy, retiring one in the lot.

"Every last one," he whispered back. "Have to be to survive in this family."

In a daze, Melissa watched as the rest of Del's family filed in to the apartment. First to come in after Gina, not counting Krys and Jennifer, were Drew and his wife, a very glowing, very pregnant young woman named Heather. Melissa felt an immediate camaraderie with the woman.

"Tony, Joe, bring in the chair," Gina ordered her sons, waving them forward. "The big one Papa used to sit in!"

"Tony on the left, Joe on the right." Del pointed to each in turn for Melissa's benefit as his brothers brought in the gray recliner.

"Right here for now," Gina pointed to a spot by the living room window. "Okay by you?" she asked Melissa as an afterthought.

"Sure." She was still astonished over getting a recliner, much less where it should go.

Gina turned her attention to Heather. "Now, you, sit down."

They all knew that drill-sergeant voice, even Heather. But Heather was stubborn. "But I want to help, Mama Santini."

Del, Melissa noted, was quick to intervene. He placed a hand on his sister-in-law's shoulder. "You can help by directing. That'll be a load off Ma's shoulders." He looked at his mother, as if daring her to argue the point.

"Make way, make way."

Melissa turned to see Kathleen coming in, ushering her three children into the apartment. A tall, distinguished-looking man walked behind her. Nick and Tony stepped to the side to admit everyone. Kathleen sought Del out of the crowd. "Sorry we're late."

"We just got here ourselves," Tony told her. Half a head taller than Del, his biceps bulged as he crossed his arms in front of his chest and leaned indolently against the nearest wall.

"Excuse me!" Melissa raised her voice to be heard above the din of voices. More than a dozen pairs of eyes turned her way. "I don't mean to be rude, but why are you all here?"

Del wrapped one arm around her waist. "This is called a housewarming. First we fill it, then we warm it."

Now that they had all entered, she looked at the assorted things they had brought in. It was a potpourri of furniture and accessories, and yet oddly enough, everything seemed to blend together. It was as if there was some sort of grand plan that had been behind all of it. The knickknacks meant to dress up her tiny kitchen counter. The gold-framed mirror. The cut-glass vase for the coffee table. The coffee table. Everything seemed to complement everything else. Del's family had brought enough things, including drapes that looked almost new, to aptly fill her living room, the small kitchen area and both bedrooms.

Melissa felt overwhelmed with gratitude and emotions she had trouble sorting out. She had told herself people like this didn't exist, yet here they were. Existing. She was completely at a loss how to deal with this flow of generosity from people who didn't know her, only—she was certain, glancing at Del—*of* her. "I don't know what to say."

"How about, let the games begin?" Del prompted. "Or the painting."

"Painting?" she could only echo dumbly. Out of the corner of her eye, she saw Kathleen's oldest sitting cross-legged by the portable crib, solemnly reading to Della about the little red hen and her practical encounter with corn.

"Tony's a house painter," Del explained. "You get him for free. Or actually," he tousled his brother's overly long hair, "for the money he owes me because he's such a lousy poker player."

Tony was indignantly elbowing his older brother out of the way. If this was going to be done, it was going to be done properly. He had brought his equipment and drop cloths. All he needed was for a color to be chosen.

"Hi," he mumbled at Melissa. He passed her a smartly printed brochure. "Del said you liked blue, so I brought several shades for you to choose from and—" He looked up, alert, as Melissa sniffed. He knew when a woman was about to cry on him. He'd been subjected to temperamental women before. Painting a home, he'd learned, seemed to bring that out in some people. Maybe Del had gotten his information wrong. "Hey, if you don't like blue—"

But Melissa shook her head, quickly wiping the tears from her cheeks with the back of her hand. She was afraid she couldn't say more than a few words. "If you'll excuse me."

She fled into one of the bedrooms. The one she had picked out to be hers.

Silence suddenly mushroomed. Del looked after Melissa, stunned. "Be right back," he muttered to the others as he hurried after her.

He walked into the bedroom and softly closed the door behind him. Melissa's back was to him, but he could tell she was silently crying. He wasn't certain what to do. Tears always disarmed him, making him feel at a complete loss. He knew how to handle it with his nieces and nephews. Promises of ice cream or toys usually did the trick. That and a warm hug. He figured the first two were not viable options and she'd resist the third. He was torn between wanting to give her a little time to herself and wanting to hold her. He settled for just being in the room.

Searching for words carefully, he gave her a moment to compose herself. "Look, I'm sorry if we overwhelmed you. In case you haven't noticed, I've got this tendency to kind of jump in and—"

She turned, shaking her head to stop him. "It's not that." She took a deep breath in an effort to steady her voice. It was a little low, a little raw when she spoke again. "I mean, you are rather overwhelming, all of you. But it's just that—no one's ever cared about me like this before." Her words were getting all jumbled. "I mean—" she gestured helplessly, trying to make him understand "—I feel totally engulfed."

"I can send them away."

He still didn't understand. She moved closer to him. "It's a nice engulfed. I feel part of something for the first time."

"Then these are happy tears?" He slid his fingertip along her cheek and brushed one aside. The idea of someone crying because they were happy mystified him.

"Yes."

His fingertip was wet. He pretended to examine it

closely. "Hard to tell the difference. They all look alike."

She did love him. It didn't change things from the way they were, the way they had to be. But she did love him. "You know, you really are a big idiot," she told him fondly.

Easily his arms slid around her. He wondered how long he had before someone would come knocking to see how she was. Not nearly long enough. "You've been talking to my mother again."

She rested her cheek against his chest. It felt so good to have him here. She'd put it all in perspective later, when her head was clearer. For now, she was just grateful. "How am I ever going to repay everyone?"

He couldn't resist brushing a kiss on her hair. "Favors come up from time to time. They'll think of something. Don't be so obsessive about paying back."

She raised her head to look at him. Was he serious? "Obsessive?" she echoed with a laugh. "Isn't that something like the pot calling the kettle black?"

He grinned in response. "When the pot's bigger than the kettle—" he drew her in closer still, noticing how well her hips seemed to fit against his "—he gets to call the kettle anything he wants."

She heard the din from the other room. For a moment, as desire flared through her body, she'd almost forgotten about them. "If they're going to stay and paint and arrange their own furniture and do who knows what, the least I can do is feed them."

Tony, Del knew, was restlessly waiting for Melissa to make a decision about which color she preferred. Once that was settled, they'd start rolling in earnest. The apartment could be painted in a few hours if they all pitched in. The place would really become a whirl-wind of activity then. "Not with my mother around, you don't. She's already called Uncle Fazio."

"Ah." Melissa's mouth almost watered. "Pizzas."

Del raised a finger to accentuate his point. "And submarine sandwiches the likes of which you've never tasted."

She began to laugh. The feeling of being over-whelmed was mellowing into one of contentment. It would be so very, very easy to believe in good things again. If only she wasn't who she was and hadn't lived through what she had. If she hadn't seen reality with her own eyes, over and over again, she could really believe that things would always remain this way.

But she did know better.

For now, though, she would walk in this wonder-land that Del and his family created and pretend that the last page hadn't already been written and was just waiting for her to turn to it.

She linked her fingers with his and walked into the living room.

Everyone turned in her direction when she entered, conversations temporarily suspended. Melissa flushed self-consciously.

"So, you're all right?" Gina took Melissa's chin in her hand and examined her face carefully.

Melissa couldn't shake the impression of a mother hen inspecting her chick after it had been rescued from a possible hawk-napping.

Gina's hand felt incredibly gentle and smooth, Melissa thought. It was a hand that had been raised more in a display of love than in a display of temper. She thought of her own mother's hand and cringed. It had never stroked, never soothed, only struck. Melissa saw the look of concern on Gina's face. "Just a little postpartum depression," she murmured.

"Ah." The expression on Gina's face told Melissa that the woman saw right through her, but she left the matter alone. "Better now?" Gina glanced at Del over Melissa's head.

"Better," they both answered the older woman at the same time.

"Good." With a sweep of her hand, Gina commandeered Melissa away from Del. Tucking her hand around Melissa's waist, Gina turned the young woman toward the furniture her sons had brought in. End tables and nightstands were piled on top of a sofa. A mattress was filling up the doorway. "So, it's time we made this into a home. You just tell the boys where you want everything and they'll do the rest. Speak slowly, they're not too quick, but they've got strong backs."

"Hey, get this damn thing out of the way!" Tony yelled from the other side of the mattress.

"As soon as you pick up your end, brother," Nick called back. "I'm an accountant, not a circus strongman."

Muttering came from behind the other end of the doorway as the obstructing mattress was raised and worked into the room.

Behind her, Melissa heard Kathleen yelling at one of her sons to stop chasing his sister. Someone had brought in an old radio and had turned it to an oldies station. Del, she realized, catching his eyes. He winked at her and her stomach responded with a flip-flop on cue. The apartment was filled to overflowing with raised voices and noise.

And Melissa had never felt so much love around her in her life.

How different all this was from her own house when she was growing up. Or Aunt Julia's, where everyone toed a straight line or suffered the consequences. Aunt Julia had been very quick with a cutting word or a strap. There'd been no love in either home, only grief and fear.

She realized Del was trying to get her attention.

"Doorbell," Del yelled, pointing. He was closer, but his path was blocked by Drew and Dennis and the kitchen table and chairs they had just brought in.

Nodding, Melissa wove her way to the doorway. The door was open, so she couldn't understand why whoever it was didn't just walk in. Everyone else in Del's family did that. Walked right into her life, she thought with a smile that was getting harder and harder to suppress.

A thin, gray-haired man with a wispy, drooping mustache that bracketed his full mouth and trickled off to his chin stood in her doorway. He wore a work shirt rolled up to the elbow and baggy gray trousers. And he was obviously studying her.

"Yes?" she prompted, wondering who he was and what he wanted. Was he drawn to all the noise? Or was he a neighbor, here to complain about it?

An appreciative smile had the mustache spreading to the old man's cheeks. "So you're the one."

"I beg your pardon?"

The old man nodded. The gleam in his eye gave him an almost devilish appearance. "No wonder his eyes shine so lately."

"Do I know you?" she asked dumbly. Of course she didn't, but he seemed to know her.

"Not me, just my pizzas." He nodded behind him toward something she couldn't see because of all the cars that were parked, blocking the area. "I delivered them myself this time so I can get a look at what all the excitement is about. Don't blame him. If I were mebbe twenty years younger, I'd be excited myself." The dark, lively eyes slid up and down her body swiftly, taking every curve into account like a man who had been doing this sort of thing most of his life. "Mebbe just ten," he amended with a sly wink.

It suddenly dawned on her. "You're Uncle Fazio."

He struck his chest with the flat of his hand. "That's me." Placing a hand on either arm to hold her steady, Fazio Santini kissed each cheek in turn. "Delighted to meet you." He released her. "Hey, which of you boys is going to earn your lunch?" he called out to his nephews.

He didn't lack for volunteers. Suddenly all activity

stopped and Melissa was surrounded by most of the members of Del's family as they responded to Fazio's call.

"Where's the truck?" Drew asked eagerly.

"Out by the curb in the front. Too many cars back here for me to park." Fazio threw Drew the keys. Drew caught them easily as they sailed over his wife's head. "Baseball," Fazio said to Melissa with a sad shake of his head. "I always said that boy should go into baseball. That's where the real money is." He frowned. "Not trading words with men in monkey suits all day."

Melissa looked up at Del for an explanation. "Drew's just become a lawyer," Del told her, laying a proprietary hand on her shoulder.

She liked the feel of that, liked the feel of all of this. Of belonging. If only it could last.

"Eh, genius, you leave my sons alone." Gina warned, hitting Fazio's chest with the back of her fingertips as three of her sons hurried past her to Fazio's truck. "Just cook."

"Ha! Sisters-in-law." Fazio waved a dismissing hand at Gina as he looked at Melissa. "Who needs them?"

"You do, old man." Bracing her hand on an arm that was still firm, still sinewy, Gina stood on her toes and brushed a kiss against his grizzled cheek. "You forgot to shave today."

Fazio made a face. "I didn't forget. I didn't want to."

"You should have a wife," Gina muttered at him

as she went out to see what else she could bring inside the apartment.

"I had a wife," Fazio called after her. "Two of them. Is it my fault they died?"

"You fed them too much," Gina tossed over her shoulder, always getting in the last word.

Muttering, he stomped after his sister-in-law to see if he could help.

Melissa shook her head. It felt as if it were spinning from all the commotion. "Are they always like this?" Melissa asked Del who was still standing next to her.

"No. This is a good day." He grinned at her. "Hey, let's make use of the reprieve. I want to show you something." Taking her hand, he carefully snaked his way past a bureau that Dennis and Joe were bringing in. "Be right back," he promised them.

Right now, he had something more important on his mind, something he wanted to give her.

Melissa glanced at Della as she followed Del into what was to be her room. Della was asleep. Incredible. Melissa grinned to herself. The noise didn't seem to bother the baby. On the contrary, Della fit right in.

"Wouldn't it be nice, baby?" she whispered.

Del tugged on her hand impatiently and she turned her attention back to him. "What?"

"This."

She looked. "This" was standing on a small desk against the wall. The desk hadn't been there when she was in the room the last time. Nor had what was on it. She looked at Del, then back at what he had brought her in to see. Her lashes felt thick as she blinked several times to hold back the tears.

Del watched her carefully. He could almost feel the throb of emotion passing through her. "It was mine," he explained. "It's not the best, but Uncle Fazio got it for me when I graduated eighth grade." He crossed to the desk. "It's been in one garage after another for years. But it still plays." As if to emphasize the point, Del lifted the arm on the old record player. "Took a lot of doing, but I finally found a store that still sells these needles. This should last you awhile." She wasn't saying anything. The silence was beginning to make him uncomfortable. "So you can play your records instead of just carrying them around," he added. Del lifted her chin. "You're not going to cry, are you?"

She shook her head, but even as she did so, a tear slid down her cheek.

"I didn't do it to make you cry." He was beginning to feel helpless again. "Is this another good tear?"

She threaded her arms around his neck, her body fitting against his. A haven. A temporary one, but a haven nonetheless. "A very good tear."

"As long as I know," he murmured, just before his lips closed the last remaining gap between them.

"If you wanna get some pizza, you'd better stop that yucky kissing stuff!" Jimmy announced as he bounced into the bedroom. A huge slice was in his hand, threatening to christen the beige carpet any second with thick sauce and mozzarella cheese.

Reluctantly Del released Melissa and grabbed the slice from Jimmy.

"Hey!" the boy protested.

"I'm just holding it for you, Jim. Tell your mom to get you a plate."

"I don't have plates," Melissa suddenly remembered.

"Sure you do," Del assured her. "Second box to your left on the kitchen counter as you walk in."

Who was she to argue?

Melissa let him take her hand and draw her back into the hub of the crowd.

Chapter Twelve

"Someone to see you, Santini," Adam Phelps, Larry's tall, angular partner called into the locker room.

Del sighed. He'd just finished changing and just wanted to get home, such as it was these days. He wasn't in the mood for any extra problems that might have wandered into the precinct in the last few minutes.

It had been just a week since Melissa and Della had moved out. It felt more like a year. He hadn't been able to see Melissa since Sunday. Work, both his and hers, kept getting in the way. Kathleen had been giving him daily reports. All was going well for mother and child, but that didn't ease any of his pain. He had found it increasingly difficult to cope with having his life back the way it had been before he had met Melissa. It didn't feel right anymore. When he returned home at night, everything was just where he had left it that morning. Including the emptiness.

Especially the emptiness.

Del looked in Phelps's direction. The thin man still stood in the doorway. "I'm off duty, Adam."

Phelps grinned. It encompassed most of his face. Larry and Phelps made Del think of Laurel and Hardy. "I think you might want to go back on for this one."

Del crumpled his uniform and shoved it into his bag. Reluctantly, a resigned scowl on his face, he went to find out what this was all about.

Phelps scratched the thinning hair at the crown of his head. "Never seen Santini this irritable before," he commented to Larry, making his voice intentionally loud enough for Del to hear.

Larry nodded his head sagely. "A woman'll do that to you."

Phelps began to change into his civilian clothing. A button pinged onto the door and he muttered under his breath. "Yeah. Every time," he agreed.

"Hey, Del," Larry called after him. "Come by the house for dinner tomorrow night. Edie has this girlfriend visiting from out of town. She'd be more than happy to fix you up." Larry raised and lowered his bushy brows comically. "You never know."

Del shook his head, impatiently shifting his sports bag to his other hand. But he did know. That was exactly the problem. He knew what he needed, *who* he needed. He just didn't know how to go about getting her. "Thanks, Larry, but I don't want to get fixed up. I'm just fine the way I am."

Or, at least he had been, before Melissa. He wanted

to stop by to see how she was doing, but he had promised himself to give her some breathing space. She needed to get adjusted to being on her own.

And it was killing him.

Secretly he hoped that she missed him and was having second thoughts about this independent life she wanted to forge for herself. He didn't want to stifle her independence. He'd let her be as independent as she wanted to, as long as she sat across from him at the breakfast table. As long as when he reached out in the middle of the night, she was there.

Del walked into the squad room, ready to be polite but short with whomever it was who wanted to talk to him. He wanted to get home, to take a really hot shower and then get himself lost in that new mystery he'd picked up for himself the other day. Anything to get his mind off Melissa.

He stopped dead at the entrance.

She was sitting in the middle of the room, in a chair next to Darcy's desk. Like a fresh rose wrapped in lavender tissue. He felt his kneecaps melting.

Melissa watched Del as he entered the room. She'd sensed his presence as soon as he had appeared in the doorway. It was as if she were suddenly gifted with a sixth sense as far as he was concerned. It was a silly thought, but she *had* known it was him before she'd looked his way. A moment earlier she'd been reading a Wanted poster on the opposite wall. And then she had just known he was there, looking at her.

She watched as he walked toward her. "Hi."

"Hi." Dropping his sports bag next to her chair,

Del leaned against the edge of the desk. What was she doing here? Stubborn as she was, he could think of only one thing that would bring her. He stopped savoring the sight of her and became concerned. "Something wrong with Della?"

"No." Did he think that was the only reason she'd come to see him? Did he think she turned her back on her obligations so easily? Didn't he have the slightest idea that he had been on her mind, waking and sleeping for the past five long days? "Della's fine. She's never been better. Kathleen's wonderful with her. She's still there right now." Melissa rose, holding her purse to her. "I came by to give you this."

Del looked down at the money she had shoved into his hand. Fifty dollars.

"I know it's not much," she said quickly, "but it's a start." She bit her lower lip. "At this rate, I'll be paying you off for a long time."

He didn't want her money, didn't want her feeling that she owed him some kind of monetary compensation because he had let her stay under his roof for such a short while. He should have been paying her for that. It had been one of the happiest experiences of his life, late-night baby-crying sessions and all. But he knew Melissa needed to do this in order to rebuild her own integrity.

"Good, then I'll have something to look forward to. And, because I've just had a sudden windfall—" he rubbed the bills together in his hand with his thumb and forefinger "—I'd like to take you out for dinner to celebrate your first full week at work."

She laughed and shook her head. He was still the same. She found a secret pleasure in that. "Don't hang on to money very long, do you?"

"Not if I can spend it on a beautiful woman." He shoved the bills into his pocket and leaned against the desk again. He found it amusing that Melissa was completely oblivious to the fact that she was turning heads all around the squad room. "I suppose I could just arrest you and take you into custody, but I'm giving you a chance to say yes of your own free will."

He didn't have to go to such lengths. She wanted to be with him. And dinner out was safe enough. "What about Della?"

He grinned. "She says yes, too. She likes me."

And so does her mother, she added silently.

Glancing at her watch she said, "I mean, I have to pick her up." She had told Kathleen her errand would take an extra half hour tonight. She was already late.

"And deprive Kathy of her company so soon? Heartless woman." He reached behind him and found the phone. "I'll call Kathy and tell her you had an emergency come up."

"What emergency?"

He grinned and dialed. "Me."

Melissa knew it would be useless to protest. She didn't want to try.

She had missed him.

* * *

He took her to a seafood restaurant that had a Hawaiian islands ambience, affordable lobster and soft, stirring music. Del was counting on the music.

"So how do you like it?" He toyed with his drink, hardly tasting it. He watched her nibble on an appetizer and relived the feel of her lips against his. He was going to drive himself crazy soon, he thought. It was only a matter of time.

The last bit of jumbo shrimp disappeared between her lips. "It's delicious."

"I meant the job."

She hesitated, then picked up another appetizer. He wasn't eating, she noticed, and wondered if he was ill. "Hectic. But I love it. I've always loved teaching. And children." Working, being on her own, gave her a huge feeling of satisfaction. But it didn't fill in all the corners. Not since she'd met Del.

He took a long sip of his scotch and soda. It was warm in his throat. Too bad it couldn't hit his heart that way. He set the glass down again. "Speaking of children, is she driving yet?"

"Who?"

"Della. Your daughter."

So he had missed them. She hugged that to her. "Del, it's only been five days." *Five very long days.*

"That's five lifetimes if you're a fruit fly."

She laughed. He'd made his point. "You can come visit her anytime you want, you know." It was a safe way of saying that she wanted him to come over. Just a mutual affection for the baby, nothing more.

"How about her mother?" Del leaned closer. So

close that he could have touched her lips with his without effort. The effort part came in restraining himself. "Can I come visit her mother anytime I want, too?"

Melissa felt her heart thud against her ribs. She drew her eyes away from his mouth. "Yes."

"Tonight?"

The hard pounding of her heart was joined by all her pulse points as desire warred with fear. If she said yes, if she let him come tonight, they both knew where that would lead. "Del, don't rush me."

"Sorry, it's in the blood." He tore a chunk of bread from the loaf the waiter had brought. He wasn't certain if he wanted to eat it or use it for therapy. He pulled a smaller piece off and chewed on it carefully. "Rome would have been built in a day if it had been up to my family. Ma's a firm believer in not letting grass grow under your feet."

The waiter arrived and cleared away the empty appetizer dish, setting down their salads in its place. She waited until the man left. "Nothing'll grow if you hurry it too much."

Del shrugged. "Patience is one of the virtues I lack, but I'll work on it." As far as he saw, he had no choice. But he would, he promised himself. Soon.

She smiled, cupping his cheek with her hand because she couldn't resist touching him any longer. "It's probably the only virtue you lack."

It only took a quick movement to bring her fingertips to his lips. He kissed each slowly, lightly, feathering desire through her and making her nerves hum. "Am I up for canonization?"

"Pretty nearly." It took effort to say that when her pulse was scrambling madly.

"Sister Margaret Mary'll probably be very happy to hear that." He found that he had to work at keeping his voice steady. He wanted her so badly he could hardly see straight. "She figured I was destined for the other place."

Her eyes almost fluttered closed. The touch of his lips, silky and smooth, was stirring erotic feelings within her. "Sister Margaret Mary doesn't know you the way I do."

"Let's hope not."

She slipped her hand into her lap. It was safer there. A lot safer. "Kathleen called you Saint Francis of Assisi the first time I met her."

He chuckled. "She was probably referring to the rustic atmosphere that the house was always in before you rolled up your sleeves and dug me out from under all that mess."

"I don't think so."

"So—" he leaned on his elbow, trying to absorb every movement, every nuance, storing it up for the long, lonely night ahead "—if I'm Mr. Terrific, why are we having such trouble moving this relationship along?"

She kept her eyes on her plate, pushing the salad around with her fork, searching for the right words. He deserved to know. "You have to understand."

"Melissa, I've been trying nothing else but, but I

need some more clues here, some input. Otherwise, I've got to assume that it's me."

"Oh, no." She reached out, her hand covering his. "It's not you. It's me." She closed her eyes, pulling herself together, trying to distance herself from the words, yet not being able to. Never being able to. The words were about the painful world she had existed in. When she spoke, her voice was husky. "All my life, I've just stood there and watched everyone leave me."

He wanted to protest, to tell her that what was in the past had nothing to do with now. With him. But this had to be said, once and for all, so it could be put behind them. He remained silent.

"First my father. He left when I was eight. Just walked out and never once looked back. I didn't even know that he was dead until over a year after he'd died. My cousin found it in an obituary column while doing research for a term paper." She bit her lip to keep it from trembling. He had been hardly more than a stranger, but he'd been her father. And it had hurt. "Then my mother left. Physically in her all-night drinking binges and then emotionally as she withdrew more and more into her depression until she was finally institutionalized. She died there."

He didn't want her dragging this up, hurting this way. "Melissa—"

She shook her head as she clenched her hands into fists. "Let me finish. I won't be able to get this out if I stop." She took a deep breath. "And finally—finally Alan." Her lips curved ruefully. "I thought he was everything I ever wanted. Light, happy. Everything was a game to him. Even my love. The day he ran out on me was supposed to be our wedding day." She looked down at her napkin. She had shredded the navy paper into ribbons. Tossing it aside, she looked up at Del. "Now I know you're different, you're good and you're kind. I know that up here." She tapped her temple. Then her finger slid down to her heart. "But here, here there's this part of me that can't get over being afraid. It's going to take time. I need time."

"To trust me?"

"Yes." She answered slowly. "Emotionally. And to trust me."

He stared. "You?"

"My judgment."

So, he'd give her time. What else could he do? He loved her. "Things do take a turn for the better, you know." He smiled at her. "Lucky streaks turn up." He took her hand. "Come on."

"Are we leaving?" They hadn't finished eating yet, she thought.

"No." He guided her past the tables. "We're dancing."

She looked over her shoulder. "But the food—"

"I have a sudden need to hold you in my arms, and for your sake, I think the least conspicuous way is if we're dancing."

Reaching the tiny dance floor, he turned to face her. "The food'll still be there when we get back. Salads are supposed to be cold."

She melted into his arms as the music drifted over them. Her body tingled just being near his. The yearning that she was trying so hard to deny throbbed throughout her, body and soul. "We're the only ones on the floor."

For him it would always be that way. "That's because we're so good." Ever so lightly, he pressed her closer, trying to absorb her into his system.

Did he really see things that way, or was he just teasing her? "No, that's because everyone else is eating. This isn't exactly inconspicuous."

"Funny, I don't notice anything." Effortlessly he moved with her as one, oblivious to the envious looks they were garnering. "Humor me." He held her close, wanting to give her his love, his comfort, wanting to chase all her demons away. Knowing what haunted her was half the battle. But only half. The rest was up to her. And with luck, to him. But it wasn't going to be nearly as fast as he wanted. He wanted it now.

Her perfume was drugging him, even as it heated his blood. "Is now a bad time to tell you I love you?"

I want to believe you, I do. I just can't. She kept her cheek against his chest, savoring the warmth, the beat of his heart. "No pressure, right?"

He lifted her chin and lightly brushed his lips against hers. "I didn't say I wouldn't fight dirty."

Her lips burned. She wanted more. Always more, and always found that there wasn't any to be had. When would she learn? "No, you didn't."

He waited, hoping. But she didn't tell him that she

loved him. He had no idea that the silence would hurt so much. He forced himself to block the pain out, telling himself that it was in her eyes. It would only take a little time before the words were on her lips as well.

He could wait.

He'd have to. He had no other choice.

She told herself in endless pep talks that she wanted no ties other than with Della. That she had to find out who and what Melissa Ryan was at this stage of her life. Sometimes, she even believed it.

Yet every time she had turned around the past two months, he was there, and she was glad even as she upbraided herself for it. Del showed up at her school during recesses to play with the children and let them sit atop his motorcycle. He gave them stern lectures about talking to strangers, and the head of the school loved him. He showed up on her doorstep on weekends to take her and Della to the zoo, to amusement parks, on picnics and to a host of other places that the baby would never remember.

But Melissa would.

He conducted a blitzkrieg.

She wanted no ties, yet they were forming, slowly, firmly, binding her. Making her feel that each day was incomplete unless she heard his voice on the phone or saw him on her doorstep, bearing flowers or pizza in his hands. He was infiltrating her mind and her soul, pushing aside the fear of desertion until it only loomed like a lone soldier in the corner.

But it was still there.

In the wee hours of the morning, when she was most vulnerable, it would leap out at her, telling her she was a fool to become so complacent. She'd been like this once before, when Alan had made her feel safe and loved. Until the morning she had woken to find him gone, to find her world gone.

She rose from her bed and watched the light rain shimmer along her windowpanes, tears feeding into one another. And remembered.

What if it happened one day with Del? What if one day he was gone? Leaving of his own volition after she gave him her love? She knew she couldn't bear it, that it would permanently destroy her, and she couldn't take that chance, couldn't risk it. If she did and it happened, then she'd be of no use to Della.

Loving, giving too much of herself, had been what had gone wrong for her mother. Her mother had been weak, had built her world completely around her father. When he left, she fell apart. Melissa pressed her forehead against the windowpane. She remembered that for a little while, Norma Ryan had tried to keep up a semblance of normalcy. She had tried putting one foot in front of the other and going on with her life. But she just hadn't been able to do it. She had felt so hurt, so betrayed, that she couldn't face life anymore. Not without her husband. Even if her daughter needed her. It hadn't been enough.

That couldn't be allowed to happen to her, Melissa vowed. She couldn't leave herself open for that to happen. As she turned back to her bed, she knew what had to be done. What she had to do if she was going to survive. She was going to have to break with Del. Leave him before he left her. There was no other way. She was growing too dependent on him. The only way she could survive was if she was the one to walk away first. It wouldn't hurt then. Not that much, at any rate.

It was the only sensible thing to do and she knew it. She had to do it now, before it was too late. Before there was no turning back.

Melissa turned her face into her pillow and cried.

Chapter Thirteen

"Hi." Del walked past Melissa into her apartment. Something was wrong. He sensed it as soon as she opened the door. He could see it in her face, in the way she stood defensively, as if she was prepared to flee. "Ready to go?"

"No."

Del sat on the sofa, feeling himself inexplicably growing tense. "You look fine to me." The matching dark green jacket and skirt were attractive on her. "But if you want to change, we've got plenty of time. I can wait." He looked at her pointedly.

She wished Della would cry, giving her an excuse to leave the room, to postpone the inevitable. But the baby had been fed and changed and was peacefully dozing. "Maybe you shouldn't."

He rose again. The sense of foreboding was becoming stifling. "We're not talking about you getting dressed for the movies, are we?" They both knew the answer to that.

"No, we're not." God, this was difficult. She hadn't realized just how difficult it was going to be until this very moment. Trying to steel herself, Melissa retrieved her purse from the kitchen table, then haltingly took out an envelope. With a burst of renewed determination, she thrust it into his hand. "Here."

Del looked at it for a long moment before opening the envelope. Inside were hundred-dollar bills. Fifteen of them. He didn't have to count to know the number. "Isn't it a little early for my pound-of-flesh payment? It's not Friday."

She swallowed. "No, it's Thursday." She was clinging to meaningless small talk when she should be trying to conclude this.

Del closed the flap. "It's also a lot more than fifty dollars. This is everything you owe me." Where did she get it? And why was it so important to pay him off? He dreaded the answer, because he thought he knew.

"Yes, it is." Melissa succeeded in making her voice sound a lot more positive than she felt. She had always felt good about tying up loose ends before. There was a triumph about not owing anyone anything.

This felt hollow.

"I took out a small loan." She flashed him a brief smile, one without any mirth behind it, as she remembered what he had said about her chances of getting

money from a bank. "It seems that some banks have
something known as a character loan." She laced her
fingers together nervously, taking care to keep a distance between Del and herself. If she got too close,
her resolve would melt. "The owner of the private
school vouched for me, and the loan officer agreed to
lend me the fifteen hundred."

He pocketed the money slowly, tucking it into his
jacket, suppressing the desire to fling it down. "So
now you owe a bank instead of me."

It sounded awful, as if she had betrayed some kind
of trust. Except that she hadn't. She was just struggling to survive, so afraid that she'd be dragged in by
the undertow. "Yes."

He studied her face carefully. "Make you feel any
better?"

"Yes," she said too quickly, then dropped her
eyes. "No."

"Multiple choice?" Because he wanted to shake
her, he shoved his hands into his pockets instead. "I'd
like to choose no."

This was hurting more than she had dreamed. Not
knowing what to do with herself, only knowing what
had to be said, she turned away from him. "Del,
maybe it's better if we don't see each other for a
while. I need time to think."

"I *have* been giving you time to think," he reminded her evenly. "Two months' worth." He
wanted to shout the words at her.

"Alone." She turned to him, a plea in her eyes. "I
can't think when I'm around you."

A smile twisted his lips. It didn't quite make it to his eyes. Desolation and dread blocked it. "I'd like to think of that as a compliment."

"I'm serious."

"So am I."

"Del, please."

He felt like snapping something in half, but there was nothing handy. Besides, it wouldn't do any good, it wouldn't change anything. Only she could do that.

He sighed loudly. "Well, there you go." He held his hands up in a gesture of surrender. When he looked at her, she could see the hurt in his eyes. "When have I ever refused you anything?" He looked toward the baby's bedroom. "Can I say goodbye to Della?"

Melissa felt heartless and cruel. Telling herself it was right and for the best didn't help at all. "She's sleeping."

Oh no, he thought, she wasn't going to deny him this, too. "Don't worry, I won't wake her. I'll use telepathy."

Any second now, she was going to cry and ruin everything. "You're not making this easy."

"Good. Because it's not exactly a picnic on this end, either." Del walked past her, trying very hard to keep his emotions under control.

He walked into the tiny second bedroom. The room was crammed with all the things Kathleen had donated from her garage. In the corner, on the floor, sat his giant teddy bear like a furry Buddha keeping vigil.

Del laughed under his breath. It was a bitter sound.

"You get to see her more often than I do," he murmured to the bear.

Careful not to wake Della, he made his way to the baby's crib. She was dressed in the pink sleepers he had bought her last week, her knees pulled in under her tummy. Long, black lashes rested like a dark crescent against her cheek. "Looks like we're going to have to wait a little while longer before we're a family, honey," he whispered to her. "Maybe a lot longer than you and I had planned."

Del frowned, frustration welling up inside of him. How could she do it? How could Melissa just turn him on and off like that? Like he was a spigot? Didn't she care at all? Had he just been deluding himself about what was between them all this time?

"It certainly looks that way, doesn't it?" he said aloud to the sleeping child.

Lightly passing his hand over the baby's head, just barely brushing the tips of his fingers along her silky black hair, Del murmured his goodbyes and then walked slowly out of the room.

Melissa was waiting for him in the living room, her fingers still laced before her, an unreadable expression on her face.

Del pressed his lips together. "So, it's don't call us, we'll call you, right?"

She couldn't stand to see him hurt this way, yet what choice did she have? "Del, please understand."

"Maybe I understand too well." His eyes narrowed as his voice grew cold. "Okay, maybe a separation *will* do us both some good." *And maybe he'd use the time to have his head examined.* ''Here's looking at you, kid.''

The door slammed behind him.

She stood staring at the door for a long, long time. It was hard to move, she discovered, when your heart was breaking.

And then Della cried, woken by the slamming door, and Melissa had something to do with herself.

But that only lasted a couple of hours. All too soon, Della was blissfully asleep again. And Melissa wasn't. She'd tried, tried for several hours, but sleep just wouldn't come. Finally she gave up and went into the living room. Still wearing nothing more than her nightgown, despite the chill in the air, she paced about the small apartment, feeling as if she was going out of her mind.

He'd left her.

Just like that. Sure she had suggested it, had pushed him to go, but she hadn't wanted him to leave. Not in her heart, not really. Melissa let out a ragged breath as she dragged her hand through her hair. She glanced into the mirror Del and one of his brothers had hung up over the sofa. She looked like a wild gypsy woman, running over the moors or wherever it was that gypsies ran, looking for her lost love.

He wasn't supposed to be lost. He was supposed to be here, with her. Oh God, what had she gone and done?

She realized now that she'd been testing him and he had flunked his finals. Miserably. By pushing him away, she had brought "someday" into being. With all her heart, she had been waiting for him to tell her that he'd never leave her, that he was here for the duration whether she liked it or not.

That he loved her too much to leave.

Instead he'd just closed the door behind him without even looking back. Easily. No, more than that. He had slammed it behind him. A sob shuddered within her. Maybe he was glad to be rid of her.

She had been right all along. She'd just precipitated the inevitable, that's all. Eventually Del would have left her just like Alan had, like her father and mother had. She'd been saved that heartache.

Except it didn't feel that way, not with this awful, lonely pain inside of her where her heart should be.

She hadn't wanted to be right. She had wanted to be proven wrong, once and for all. She wanted her happily-ever-after.

Melissa filled her lungs, trying to hold back the hot tears that were pushing their way out. The desolation that ate away at her was worse than anything she had ever gone through. There had never been any warmth between her father and her. His disappearance hadn't been a total surprise. Her mother's retreat had come in stages, so though it hurt, she had known it was coming.

And even with Alan, the signs had all been there. The late nights, the frivolous spending of money, the refusal to settle down, those had all been signs. If she had been honest with herself, if she had wanted to see, she would have seen it coming.

But Del had left no signs. Not a single trace, not a single warning. It was like a flash flood, coming out of nowhere. A part of her had begun to believe, to have hope that maybe she wasn't doomed to relive some awful pattern over and over again. That this time, the person she loved would stay. She hadn't been prepared.

She roamed around the room, straightening things up. Seized with an impatient impulse, she shoved the neatly piled magazines onto the floor, scattering them every which way. And she left them there.

Damn! She'd done this to herself. But it didn't help any, knowing that. It didn't erase the pain, didn't make it any easier knowing she was to blame.

It made it worse.

She looked at the clock on the wall. The clock was from Gina, the paint behind it from Tony. Her whole apartment was a mosaic, contributions from people who loved Del. Just like she did.

The tears spilled out and she brushed them away impatiently. It was 2:03. She was going to look like a zombie and probably frighten all the children at school tomorrow. At school *today,* she corrected herself. She had to get some sleep.

But lying down would do no good. She'd just toss and turn the way she had for the past three hours. Still, she had to try.

Her hand had just brushed against the light switch on the kitchen wall, shutting it off, when she heard the doorbell. And then the pounding.

Nervously she looked through the peephole and

saw nothing. The light by her door had gone out earlier tonight. Like the light in her life. It seemed rather appropriate at the time.

She jumped as the pounding began again, this time so hard that it vibrated through the heavy fire door.

"Open the damn door, Melissa!"

"Del?" She looked through the peephole again, straining to make out his form.

"Who were you expecting at this hour?" he shouted. "Captain Kangaroo?"

She fumbled with the dead bolt he had insisted on installing for her. She hardly had enough time to take the chain off when the door flew open, banging against the opposite wall.

He scowled at her, hands on his hips. The near-transparent nightgown she was wearing would have had him weak in the knees if he wasn't so angry. "I've been separated long enough, how about you?"

She'd never seen him this incensed before. But she didn't back away. "What?"

"I've had just about all the separation I can take. I want to know if you feel the same way." He swiped at the light switch with the flat of his hand. The fluorescent light in the kitchen went on as he turned around. That was when he saw them. The tracks of her tears, glistening in the light. Something twisted inside him.

"Yes," he said, touching her face, tracing the path of one tear. "I think you have."

She threw herself into his arms and cried with relief. The sobs shook her entire body.

"Hey, hey." Overwhelmed, confused, Del stroked her hair, trying to sort out her sudden change in behavior. "What's the matter?"

It felt so good to be held. So wonderful to inhale that manly scent that was his alone. "I thought you were gone."

"I was," he replied. "You shoved me out through the mail slot, remember?"

She raised her head to look at him. "But you didn't have to go."

"Is this some complex female logic I'm not supposed to understand?" With his thumbs, he gently rubbed away the tearstains from her face. Then he took her by the shoulders and held her away from him, studying her face. "I need you, Melissa. I need you both. I don't want some Ivy League guy in a three-piece suit to raise Della. I want to be there for her first word, for her first steps. I want to be there to dry her first tears when she has her first heartache. I want to be her father. I *am* her father. It takes more than biology to make a father. Any kid past puberty can accomplish that. Being a father means caring. It means *wanting* to care. I care. Della was mine from the very first moment I held her, just the way you were the first moment I held you. Don't you see? I want to grow old with you." He framed her face with his hands. "And most of all, I want to love you like nobody's loved you."

"Come rain or come shine?" Though her heart was bursting, she couldn't resist completing the lyric.

He smiled. "You've heard the song."

She nodded in answer. She knew all the words, too. As she did to all the songs she had played while waiting for her mother to return.

"It was one of my mother's favorites when I was growing up," Del told her. "I never really understood the lyrics before now. I want to be with you no matter what, Melissa. And if you're waiting for me to walk out on you like Alvin—"

"Alan."

"—like that good-for-nothing jackass who abandoned you, you're going to grow very old waiting because I don't intend for that to happen. Ever." He searched her face for a hint that she comprehended what he was saying to her. "I love you. I love Della. God help me, I even love not being able to find anything because you've been so damned organized and put it all away."

He held her close again, letting himself absorb the feel of her. "Can't you see? I need the order you bring to everything around me and the chaos you bring to my insides. Marry me, Melissa, or I swear I'll put you under house arrest and appoint myself your jailer for the rest of my natural life."

"Jailer," she repeated, holding back her smile and the answer she knew she would give. The only one she could give. "Is that what you think of marriage? That it's like being in jail?"

"No, I think of marriage as something wonderful." He stroked her hair. "Now that I've found you. But I wouldn't mind solitary confinement—as long as it was with you."

"Then it wouldn't be solitary."

He raised and lowered his eyebrows the way he'd seen Larry do. "Catch on fast, don't you?" He looked over her head at the scattered magazines on the floor. "Hey, I like what you've done with the place."

She looked over her shoulder to see what he was talking about. She might have known. "I'm turning over a new leaf." Then she looked up into his eyes. "Lots of new leaves." She laughed, feeling all the tension she'd been carrying around with her for so long drain away from her. "I never had a chance, did I?"

"Nope. Never. Haven't you heard? We always get our man. Or woman."

She cocked her head slightly. "I thought you said that was just the Mounties."

He shrugged as he nipped her lower lip, running the tip of his tongue along it. He felt her shiver against him. "We're expanding. Now stop arguing with me, say yes and kiss me."

She sighed, leaning into his kiss, feeling the hot press of his body against hers. Desire flared, sharp and true. "I thought you'd never ask."

"Is that a yes?"

"That is emphatically a yes." Melissa placed her hands on his forearms, stopping him just before he kissed her again.

"More talking?" he asked suspiciously.

"Just a little."

"Make it quick. I want to kiss every square inch

of your face." He grinned wickedly. "After that, we'll play it by ear."

And she knew the tune. And welcomed it. But she needed to say this to him. "The only way I could get by at times was believing that there was something wonderful waiting for me just around the next corner. And now, there finally is."

He expected her to say something about her newly won independence. "What?"

"You."

She saw that her answer surprised him. Maybe it surprised her a little, too. Standing on her toes, her thin nightgown rubbing seductively against him, she wove her fingers into his thick hair. "You're everything I want, Del. I was just too afraid to believe that I'd finally found someone to love, someone to love me. Someone who would stay. Afraid because I've been disappointed so many times before."

His arms tightened around her protectively. "Prepare yourself never to be disappointed again."

She raised her lips to his. "I'm counting on it."

*   *   *   *   *

Bundles of Joy

Babies have a way of bringing out the love in
everyone's hearts! And this summer,
Silhouette Romance is presenting you
with two wonderful love stories.

June:

THE TYCOON'S TOTS by Stella Bagwell (#1228)

Twins on the Doorstep continues! Chloe Murdock was set to adopt
those sweet baby twins left on her doorstep—when their uncle,
Wyatt Sanders, suddenly appeared. The handsome tycoon wanted to raise
the tots as his own, but Chloe was soon hoping they'd all become part of
a full-fledged family....

August:

BABY BUSINESS by Laura Anthony (#1240)

Millionaire Clay Barton suddenly had a baby to care for—and needed
some help, fast! So when the lovely, capable Dr. Tobie Avery showed up,
Clay thought he was in the clear. That is, until Tobie's womanly charms
had this rugged daddy figure imagining the tempting pediatrician in a
more permanent position—as his wife!

Don't miss these adorable Bundles of Joy,
coming in June and August,
only from

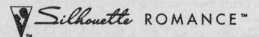

Silhouette is proud to introduce
the newest compelling miniseries by
award-winning author

SUSAN MALLERY

TRIPLE TROUBLE

Kayla, Elissa and Fallon—three identical triplet sisters
are all grown up and ready to take on the world!

✳✳✳✳✳✳✳✳✳✳✳✳✳✳✳✳✳✳✳✳

In August: **THE GIRL OF HIS DREAMS
(SE#1118)**

Could it be Prince Charming was right in front of her
all along? But how was Kayla going to convince her
best friend that she was the girl of his dreams?

In September: **THE SECRET WIFE
(SE#1123)**

That Special Woman Elissa wasn't ready to throw in
the towel on her marriage, and she set out to show
her husband just how good love could be the second
time around!

In October: **THE MYSTERIOUS STRANGER
(SE#1130)**

When an accident causes her to wash up on shore,
the handsome man who finds her has no choice but to
take in this mysterious woman without a memory!

Don't miss these exciting novels...only from

Silhouette®SPECIAL EDITION®

FOR BETTER... FOR WORSE... FOR A WEEK

The seven days that turned two couples' lives topsy-turvy!

A darling Yours Truly duet by
HAYLEY GARDNER

THE ONE-WEEK WIFE
June 1997

A baby left on a doorstep...which results in a
one-week battle-of-the-sexes bet on whether
a man or a woman can take better care of
little Teddy. All's fair in war...and love!

THE ONE-WEEK BABY
July 1997

A pretend wife for a week...which results in
a next-door-neighbor romance that is
anything but neighborly. Pretending isn't half
as much fun as the real thing....

Heat up your summer with short,
sassy love stories from
Hayley Gardner and Yours Truly.
Romance has never been hotter!

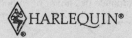

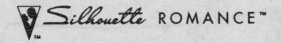

Silhouette ROMANCE™

What's a single dad to do when he needs a wife by next Thursday?

Who's a confirmed bachelor to call when he finds a baby on his doorstep?

How does a plain Jane in love with her gorgeous boss get him to notice her?

From classic love stories to romantic comedies to emotional heart tuggers, **Silhouette Romance** offers six irresistible novels every month by some of your favorite authors! Such as...beloved bestsellers **Diana Palmer, Annette Broadrick, Suzanne Carey, Elizabeth August** and **Marie Ferrarella,** to name just a few—and some sure to become favorites!

Fabulous Fathers...Bundles of Joy...Miniseries... Months of blushing brides and convenient weddings... Holiday celebrations... You'll find all this and much more in **Silhouette Romance**—always emotional, always enjoyable, always about love!

SR-GEN

WAYS TO *UNEXPECTEDLY* MEET MR. RIGHT:

♡ Go out with the sexy-sounding stranger your daughter secretly set you up with through a personal ad.

♡ RSVP yes to a wedding invitation—soon it might be your turn to say "I do!"

♡ Receive a marriage proposal by mail— from a man you've never met....

These are just a few of the unexpected ways that written communication leads to love in Silhouette Yours Truly.

Each month, look for two fast-paced, fun and flirtatious Yours Truly novels (with entertaining treats and sneak previews in the back pages) by some of your favorite authors—and some who are sure to become favorites.

YOURS TRULY™:
Love—when you least expect it!

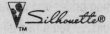